QUARTERBACK SNEAK

BAYLIN CROW

SERIES NOTE

While there is a real Sugar Land, Texas, the fictional city this book takes place in is simply that. Fictional. Each story in the Sugar Land Saints Series will be semi-standalone and each will focus on a new couple. You can read them separately, but I recommend reading them in order. Characters from previous books in the series will make appearances and be referenced while new characters for future books will also be introduced.

Hope you enjoy!

Baylin xo

ONE

RUSH

MUSIC BLARED from a truck's speaker system as we sat around a crackling bonfire. The chatter of friends droned in the background and some danced to the pounding beat. Sweat dotted my brow, even as the late fall breeze cooled my back.

The smell of burning wood drifted through the air as I took a pull of my beer, the bitter liquid coating my tongue before sliding down my throat.

My best friend, Torin, and I sat in matching weathered folding chairs with a small blue and white cooler on the ground between us. I'd snagged my uncle's beer from the mudroom refrigerator and then driven us the short distance to the open field behind an abandoned farm.

Every year during bye week the team got together. It was tradition, and we were supposed to spend it like family, bonding or whatever. I glanced around at the scene and sighed. While Torin and I never did, most of the guys brought girlfriends, or buddies, completely disregarding the reason for the night. It almost made me question why we bothered. But in small town Texas, you didn't mess with football traditions. Even the cops looked the other way, knowing damn well there were minors with alcohol.

As seniors, Torin and I had bigger things to focus on. We were both being heavily scouted by colleges all over the US, but we both had our hearts set on staying in Texas and close to our families.

The rusted metal chair next to me creaked and groaned as Torin leaned forward in it, resting his elbows on his knees as he sipped his beer. He considered the can in his hand with a look of disgust. "This stuff is nasty."

The corner of my lip kicked up. It was one of the worst things I'd had the displeasure of tasting but swallowed another mouthful anyway. I shrugged as I leaned back in my chair, dangerously balancing on the back two legs.

"It was the best I could do." While my parents wouldn't buy it for me, if they discovered I'd taken it, they'd turn a blind eye like everyone else in town. As long as I threw him some cash, I doubted my uncle would care. "Beggars can't be choosers, T."

A small six-pack was all I managed and I shared with Torin because, well, we'd always shared everything. He'd been my best friend since Mrs. Carmine's Pre-K class when we discovered we shared a birthday. And then our mutual love of football cemented our friendship forever.

"Well, your uncle has bad taste." Despite his words, he brought the can to his generous lips again and then he grinned, flashing his straight white teeth.

My gaze roamed over his familiar face, tan skin, cobalt-blue eyes that glowed from the flames, messy blond hair that stuck out from under his hooded sweatshirt. I studied the face of the boy I'd been in love with for as long as I could remember. The face of the man I still did.

His smile faded as he stared back at me intensely. "What?"

"Nothing." I cleared my throat and chuckled uneasily. "It's the cheap stuff and since he's sleeping on our couch, I don't think he has much money. Although I don't doubt he also has bad taste."

Torin frowned as he worked the tab of his beer back and forth until it broke off. "I wonder what his deal is anyway."

"No idea. My parents still haven't said anything other than his girlfriend kicked him out and he needed a place to crash." I'd only met the guy one other time and it was a little odd to have him in our house still, three weeks after he showed up on our doorstep.

"Don't know how long he'll stay?"

"Nope." The word popped on my lips.

Though a cold front had come through the day before, the fire was just too hot. I was dressed in track pants and a t-shirt and sweating my ass off. I took my hat off, letting the cool wind that swept through the surrounding tall grass ruffle my short brown hair. At the same moment Torin shivered. While I was always hot, he was always cold. Once the sun had set, the temperature had dropped a few degrees, adding more bite to the night air.

"Are you cold?" I planted the front two legs of my chair back safely on the ground and slouched down, crossing my ankles in front of me.

Torin reached down between our chairs, breaking eye contact, and tossed his empty can in the cooler before grabbing another. "I'm okay."

Ready to argue with him about leaving, I opened my mouth, but he spoke first.

"So how are you feeling about this season?" he asked while popping the tab of his third beer.

I'd spent the last year working out and bulking up as much as possible. Being six-six and weighing much more than most of the guys, I played my position well. Though my build wasn't typical of a center because I carried my weight in solid muscle, I was large and immovable. Torin had started as a quarterback when we were kids and the role stuck. I liked that we worked as a unit. We always played on the same team, me being the one who snapped the ball to him each play and the first in line to protect him from our opponents. It was a job I took seriously.

I placed my cap back on my head and adjusted the bill. "Honestly, I'm in the best shape I think I possibly could be. Maybe playing the best ball I ever have. I hope the scouts like what they see."

A choked sound left Torin's throat and once again I faced him, meeting his amused expression.

"I didn't mean you. You're perfect." His crooked grin made an appearance as a lump lodged itself in my throat. He tipped his chin toward a small group of younger Varsity members. "I meant them. Do you think they'll carry the team well when we leave next year?"

"I mean they might have a hard time replacing us." I winked at him and he rolled his eyes. "But I think they'll be all right."

"Yeah, you're right. It's just going to be weird leaving this behind, but I'm excited too. You know? I guess it's just now really hitting me." He stood, rising to his full six feet and held his beer out. "Hold this? I'll be right back."

After he'd handed me his can, he headed for the tree line and my gaze drifted to his backside encased in a pair of stonewash jeans that molded his ass to perfection. It wasn't the first time I checked Torin out and it wouldn't be the last.

I couldn't stop if I tried, and I had. It was distracting in the worst way.

I wasn't in denial. My attraction to Torin went deeper than the beautiful surface and my feelings for him were well beyond the boundaries of friendship. Though he knew I was bisexual, he never brought it up and it didn't seem to bother him. But he definitely wasn't and had girlfriends off and on in the past. It was just the way things were and to keep him in my life it was something I had to deal with.

So I had. I'd had girlfriends, but never a boyfriend. Even though both of my parents knew I was into both women and men, I wasn't ready to make it common knowledge. I also didn't think it would be fair to date anyone when my heart was completely invested in one person already.

Sighing, I tilted my head back and finished my beer before throwing it in the cooler and closing the lid. The drive home would be short but my limit was two.

"Rush."

I heard my name and glanced around until I spotted Brian, another senior, trying to get my attention. "What's up?"

"See the brunette over by Cassie?" He tilted his head toward his girlfriend who danced with a girl I didn't recognize. She wore a dress that floated up every time she spun around, showing everyone more than her moves. "She's into your boy, Torin. Thought he might appreciate easy pickings. Where'd he go?"

He glanced over my shoulder and my fist balled. I had to remind myself if I didn't want to be suspended, I couldn't hit him.

"Here and not interested." Torin's smooth voice came from behind me with a note of disgust that echoed the roll of my stomach. He approached my side and took his beer I was holding and poured it out on the ground. "I think I'm ready to leave."

"Really?" Brian asked with a look of disbelief. "She's only visiting for a week before she goes home. Hell, she lives in a different state—"

"Not interested," Torin repeated calmly before returning his attention to me. "You ready?"

"Let's go," I agreed and stood, giving Brian my back.

We said our goodbyes and then collected our two chairs and cooler before we carried them to my truck parked only a few yards away. We tossed the chairs into the back before I drained the melted ice onto the ground and slid it in beside them.

When I climbed in the driver's seat, Torin was already in the cab with his head leaning on the window.

"Everything all right?" I asked while I pulled my keys from my pocket and then cranked the engine. The old beat-up frame rattled when the engine roared.

He faced me with a tired grin. "Yeah, just sleepy. You mind if I stay over?"

"Why would I mind? You stay over all the time or I'm at your place." I had to drive in a giant circle in the field before I could get back on the rocky road and head toward home.

When I glanced over, Torin shrugged. "Just making sure."

Confused, but blaming it on a random odd moment, I let it go.

My parents' house sat on ten acres, a small ranch-style home surrounded by mud, grass and tall green trees. There was a small pond and a run-in shed where my mom's appaloosa mare, Lucy, rested for the night.

I drove down the long driveway, a mixture of grass and rock. After pulling around back, I parked next to the giant oak tree with an old tire swing still hanging from a branch though no one used it.

Torin and I got out of the truck and he stopped by the tailgate. "Should we take this stuff inside?"

I waved him off. "I'll get it in the morning."

It was already past midnight and a shower before crawling into bed sounded like pure bliss.

We entered through the back door, depositing our shoes in the mudroom and I peeked around the corner. Mom and Dad's door down the hall was closed and the glow from the TV lit up my uncle's tall sleeping form stretched out on the couch. Torin and I crept down the opposite hall to my room. Once the door shut behind us, I began to rid my pockets of my phone, wallet and keys onto my unfinished wood dresser. Torin did the same, setting his things next to mine.

"Do you mind if I grab a shower first?" he asked as he started to lift his shirt.

Deliberately not glancing his way, I waved in his general direction. "Go for it."

The en-suite bathroom door clicked shut behind me before the sound of the shower turning on filtered through the door.

I tugged my shirt over my head and then pulled my pants off before picking them up and shoving them in the laundry basket in the corner. A loud thud came from the other side of the bathroom door that sounded like something heavy getting knocked over followed by Torin's curse.

"Rush," he called before I could ask if he was all right.

"Yeah?" I called back.

When there was no answer, I sighed and went to the door. Cracking it open, I found Torin with his head stuck around the curtain.

"Can I borrow something to wear? The blue shorts?"

He still had shampoo in his hair and I bit back a grin. "Give me a minute."

Torin borrowed my clothes often enough that I was tempted to start his own section in my closet. I retreated to my room and dug around until I found the blue pair of drawstring shorts he could tighten around his leaner waist before taking them back to the bathroom.

When I opened the door I didn't expect him to be out of the shower, much less naked and running a towel over his body. His long, thick cock hung between his toned thighs and I bit back a groan. After having gawked at him a beat too long, I spun around and held the shorts out behind me. "Sorry, man. I didn't hear the water turn off."

He took them from me. "It's cool."

But it wasn't. I didn't want him to think I'd done that on purpose, but I wasn't in a position to express my concerns. My boxer-briefs grew tight as my cock continued to swell as all my blood rushed south. Needing to make an escape, I bolted back into my room and busied myself, packing my gear for the next day and then grabbing clean underwear.

I waited for him to come out before passing him, careful not to brush against him, and then locked myself in the bathroom where I took several deep breaths until I gained control and then climbed into the shower. My cock was still half hard and the temptation to wrap my hand around my shaft to get off was strong. Though I'd had weak moments in the past, I didn't want to do it to the thought of my best friend, especially when he was just on the other side of the door. It felt like I was betraying him.

My shower was quick and efficient before I brushed my teeth and slipped on my underwear. Glancing at myself in the mirror, I ran a hand over my short wet hair. Hazel eyes, olive skin and sharp features stared back at me as I gave myself a mental pep talk. *He's your best friend. Stop thinking about his fucking cock.*

Satisfied and confident that the situation was under control, I picked up my towel and exited the bathroom. Torin was curled up on my king size bed that was nearly too small for me, his eyes still open and watching me.

"What?" I asked as I tossed my towel in the basket and noticed that he had too.

His gaze slid down my body like a gentle caress, but I knew I was seeing things that weren't there.

"Do you ever..." He licked his lips. "I've been thinking. Do you ever wonder..."

When he paused again, my brow furrowed. I hit the lights and in the dark, circled to my side of the bed before peeling back the already messy comforter. Sliding between the sheets, I got comfortable on my side, facing Torin's back. "Do I ever wonder what?"

I yawned and settled in, waiting for him to confide in me whatever was on his mind. Only a moment passed before the mattress springs creaked under Torin's weight as he rolled over. He edged toward me, his body heat growing warmer as he invaded my space and the spicy scent of my body wash he'd used grew stronger. His erratic breathing was deafening in the silent room and warning bells sounded in my mind.

When his leg brushed mine, I sucked in a breath. "What are you doing?"

He rested his hand on my bare chest. My breathing picked up and my dick instantly responded, perking back up.

"You can tell me to stop." His voice shook as he hesitantly touched my heated skin with fingertips roughened from football.

"Torin?" My voice was equally shaky and my mind swarmed with questions.

"Can I kiss you?" The words were so quiet, but they rang out crystal clear.

Every cell in my body froze and words eluded me. That had been the last thing I ever expected to hear.

Taking my silence as a lack of objection, Torin scooted farther into my space, pushing more of his body against mine. His touch trailed up over my pecs and around to the back of my head where he ran his fingers through my hair, and then lips that were soft and tasted of my minty toothpaste gently pressed against mine.

The sensation shocked me enough I could speak and mumbled against his mouth. "Should we be doing this?"

"I don't know."

My next words were interrupted as he slipped his tongue into my mouth and I groaned. My reservations dissolved until all I could do was feel and taste Torin. I snapped. Before I could process my next move, I flipped him onto his back and crawled on top of him. I kissed him back, massaging his tongue with mine, nipping at his lips and swallowing each of his moans.

"Rush." He panted and squirmed beneath me. "I want..."

Silencing him with another kiss, I felt him rock his hips up against mine. Unrestrained I thrust against him with the thin layers of fabric the only things that separated our hard cocks. His hands went to my ass, pulling me against him and I grunted with approval. But when his fingers slipped beneath the elastic band of my briefs, I stopped cold. What were we doing?

I rolled off of him, lying next to him and staring up into

the dark, trying to wrap my head around what had just happened. What *had* just happened?

"What's wrong?" Torin reached out and ran his finger over my lips.

Grabbing his hand, I pulled it down to my chest but still held it. "I can't be an experiment for you, T." It would destroy me when he moved on.

"You wouldn't be an experiment. What the hell?" He sounded angry.

I didn't understand. "You're straight."

He chuckled softly, his mood lightened. "Not exactly. I've thought about it before, you know? A lot. But only with you."

How had he kept a secret like that from me? Then I felt the weight of being a hypocrite. But then his words sank in and my heart raced. I opened my mouth several times before I managed to create words. "Never anyone else?"

"Not like this," he admitted and tried to rub his hand over my chest, but I gripped his hand tighter to keep him still.

So many questions buzzed heavily in my heart and mind. My world had just been upended and flashes of hope followed by disbelief seemed to be taking turns driving me mad.

"I've thought about it a lot too," I finally responded. The admission felt like a heavy burden being lifted from my shoulders.

"So, why are we stopping?" He didn't sound surprised, so I guessed I hadn't hidden my attraction as well as I'd hoped.

"If you want this... if you want me"—I took a deep breath and exhaled—"you better be damn sure. I'm not interested in a one-time thing, T."

"Who says I am? You don't get to decide that for me, Rush." The words were soft but firm.

"T, I'm serious. This just came out of the blue. I wasn't expecting it and I'm a little confused. I'm having a hard time keeping pace with you right now."

He let out a heavy sigh. "I didn't handle this well at all, did I?"

"Let's just sleep on it. I need to think and maybe you do too."

Torin leaned up and quickly pecked my lips before settling in at my side. He tossed a leg over mine and huffed. "Have it your way."

I wasn't sure how much sleep I'd get after what we'd just done but it was true that I needed to figure it out. Figure *us* out.

SOMETIME IN THE early morning hours I must have fallen asleep because I woke to whispered voices that were growing louder by the second. Torin stirred next to me and when I glanced at him, he cracked his eyes open. He squinted and tilted his head, mimicking my position as I tried to overhear the conversation.

Checking the alarm clock on my nightstand, it showed eight in the morning. It was clear there was an argument and then my uncle's voice broke through the confusion.

"There's no need to tell him." He sounded exasperated.

My interest was piqued. I scrambled out of bed, grabbing a pair of practice shorts from my closet and slipped them on. Quietly, I eased the door open to hear better.

"Keep your voice down!" my mom demanded. "John, Joel and I discussed it and we think it's time. He's eighteen now and deserves to know."

The hair on my arms stood on end. *Are they talking about me?*

"We didn't agree to this, Angela," my uncle spat. "When you said you would take care of him..."

My mom's laugh was humorless. "We didn't expect you to show up on our doorstep either."

Dad's voice boomed over the others'. "We planned on telling him anyway, but with you here maybe it's best we do it now."

My mind spun with the possibilities. I eased the door open farther and crept into the hall with Torin almost pressed against my back. We stepped lightly across the wood flooring as we drew closer to the argument concerning me and something I apparently needed to be told.

"Is this why you let me stay? Did you plan on springing this on him while I was here?" My uncle sounded like he was about to snap and that wasn't something I'd tolerate.

"What's going on?" I asked and entered the living room. All three jumped, each wearing matching expressions: guilt. My stomach tightened. "Mom? Dad?"

My gaze slid to my uncle who stared at the floor while rubbing his hand across forehead.

Mom quickly glanced at both my dad and uncle briefly and when neither would obviously help, she huffed. "Honey, maybe you ought to sit down." Her gaze slid to Torin and back. "And maybe we should have this conversation in private."

I crossed my arms over my chest, refusing to budge. "Torin stays and I think maybe I should be told what's going on."

When I felt Torin's hand on my back, I relented and let him guide me farther into the room and onto the brown leather couch. He took a seat next to me and pressed his solid thigh against mine. My mom sat on my other side while both men stood, sending each other challenging glares.

"We have something important to tell you," she began,

her hands twisting in her long skirt. "But it's important to start with telling you how much we love you. Your dad and I, our hearts were so full of love when you were born and I—"

"Mom," I cut in. "Just tell me what the hell is going on."

She didn't correct my language so I knew it was bad. She drew in an audible breath, releasing it slowly. "You're right. Okay, Rush. Uncle John, he's not your uncle." She visibly swallowed. "He's your... he's your biological father."

Without thinking, I jumped to my feet, startling my mom who jerked away. My gaze swung to each of them. "Okay, guys, not funny."

I met my dad's eyes and waited for him to confirm this was a twisted joke, but he shook his head. "Rush, you will always be my son. Period. But my brother is your biological father."

My mind spun as my world fell apart. Torin stood at my side, but even his firm grip on my arm wasn't helping. I glanced at my uncle—*Shit, my father?*—and my stomach bottomed out.

Gritting my teeth, I asked the next dreaded question. "Then who is my mom?"

Mom's face crumpled. "I am."

My vision dimmed at the edges as I became light headed. This time Torin squeezed my arm harder, grounding me while I tried to understand. "Someone please explain what the hell is going on." When the three of them traded glances again, I fumed. "You know what, never mind." I was over it. Done. I mean, *what the fuck?*

Torin was right behind me as I started for my room and my mom hurried after me.

"I told you it was a bad idea." My uncle's tone was harsh.

"Rush, wait a minute," my mom said from my doorway as I went to my closet to gather clothes for the day. I turned around and crossed my arms over my chest. "Just, please let me explain and then you can decide if you hate me."

I squeezed my eyes shut. "I don't hate you, Mom. I'm seriously confused and hurt, I guess. Nothing makes sense. Why would you and Dad lie to me about this?"

"Well, it's a complicated story, but I'd like to tell you if you're willing to hear it." When I did nothing but silently stare at her, she took that as permission to enter my room and sat on the edge of my bed, her hands went back to her skirt, twisting the fabric.

"I started dating your uncle when I was young and naïve, barely eighteen. I didn't realize he had a drug and alcohol addiction. I knew I wasn't comfortable with the crowd he ran with, but I thought he'd change once we settled down. But then I got pregnant with you. He left me alone, pregnant and desperate.

"When your dad found out what his brother had done, he started checking in on me. He took me to my doctor appointments and held my hand when we saw you for the first time on the monitor. He was with me the first time I heard your heart beat. As I fell in love with you, so did he. And he made it impossible not to love him, so we married.

"When you were born, your dad tracked down John and told him he wanted to adopt you. John readily agreed and signed the papers."

A choked sound snuck past my lips before I could smother it, and my mom's eyes welled with tears.

"He wasn't sober or interested in becoming a family man. I'm so sorry, honey." She watched me for a moment before continuing her story. "Your dad and I took the required steps and he legally became your father. But, honey, he was already your dad. He loves you so much. You were as much a gift to him as you were to me, and he always thought of you as his own. It has been killing him to imagine that you might not think of him that way anymore. But we wanted to be honest."

"Of course I still love him. He's my dad." I gave her an incredulous look. "It's just so messed up. Where were Grandma and Grandpa during all this?"

A tear slipped free and left a wet trail as it raced down her cheek. "They took a while to come around to me being an unwed mother. Your dad fixed that before it happened."

I nodded though I was lost to my own thoughts. "Why didn't either of you tell me?"

She shook her head and whispered, "We were scared."

I scrubbed my hands over my face. "I need time to think... to... I don't know. But I love you and Dad. I just need to get out of here." My gaze turned to Torin who leaned against the wall. He gave me a subtle nod.

A small sob escaped her and she covered it with a cough. She climbed to her feet and gave me a light hug. When I pulled her in tighter, she hiccupped. "I understand."

After she walked out, shutting the door softly behind her, I faced Torin and wondered what he was thinking. He studied me right back.

"Fucked up, right?" I searched his expression for pity. I didn't want that.

"Let's get out of here," he responded before turning to my closet and borrowing a pair of sweatpants and a long sleeve shirt.

I kept my shorts on and grabbed the first t-shirt I saw. After we both quickly brushed our teeth, I snatched my keys from my dresser and slung my practice bag over my shoulder.

No one was in sight as we left the house. Torin and I climbed into my truck, riding in silence as I steered us back to the clearing we'd left the night before. I turned the ignition off and stepped out, hearing his door shut right after mine. I unlatched the tailgate and then hopped up onto the rusted bed. Flopping down onto my back, the bright blue morning sky made me squint. Torin lay beside me. It had to be cold outside, but I was numb. Torin didn't even make his usual crack about my choice of outfit.

The wind whipping through the tall grass and a few noisy birds broke the silence. Torin threaded his warm fingers through mine. "Are you okay?"

"I think maybe I need to talk to him." Turning my head, I faced him. "What do you think?"

He squeezed my hand. "If you have questions, you should get them off your chest. It might help."

I agreed and planned to do that. I'd created a mountain of questions for the man who abandoned me and my mom. But when I made it home after practice that day, my uncle was gone. My mom, appearing very uncomfortable, told me that he said his girlfriend took him back, clearly a lie. He never tried to contact me again, so I was left confused and full of questions that only he could have answered. Life resumed as if an exposed secret hadn't upset my reality, except this nagging presence of loose ends kept me slightly off balance. And while I hated it, I found myself wondering about him often.

I channeled all my frustration to the game and ended up having my best season. Both Torin and I were offered scholarships to multiple colleges. Luckily, we'd both landed at Sugar Land University, close enough to home for an occasional visit, just what we'd hoped for.

The day we traded our Riverside Bulldogs' red and white jerseys for the black and gold colors of the Sugar Land Saints, I knew things would be okay. Everything felt right with my best friend by my side. I trusted Torin with my life and I'd never do anything to screw up that friendship. That kiss would have to be our first and our last. I wouldn't risk losing him.

THREE
RUSH

A SOLID WALL of yellow and green jerseys stretched in a long line, facing me and my offensive line. The Cougars' team was full of giants, rivaling the sizes of my own team-mates. Some players were as big as me, bigger even. High school was nothing compared to college ball and this team had been a beast of an opponent the entire game.

Muscles in my legs and back cramped as we neared the final minutes. With the score tied and knowing this might be our last drive of the game, we needed to put points on the board. I held the football's tip to the ground, ready to snap it backward into Torin's waiting hands at his call.

I felt, rather than saw, Torin bend down, reaching under me from behind with both hands. The noise from the crowd nearly drowned out his call. "Green 90! Ready!"

The behemoth across from me dropped into his stance. With one hand braced on the turf, he readied to spring forward the second the ball left my hand. When I stared him down, he smirked and pointed a taunting finger. Fucking asshole.

Both lines held completely still, until Torin tapped me once on the thigh signaling me. "Hut, hut!"

I snapped the ball to him and immediately sprang up. My cleats dug into the ground and I pushed against the wide chest of the man trying to get through me to reach Torin. Not fucking likely. Because of the call he'd made, I knew Torin had retreated into the pocket and was searching for either Nash or Shaw to throw to.

Trying to get around me, the guy grabbed my jersey and held tight. He was smart enough to do it where the ref couldn't see well enough to call him for holding. It almost worked and we struggled against each other until the ball went sailing over my head.

With a final shove, I disengaged and backed up, watching the long ball as it sliced through the air, targeting Nash. With one hand, the receiver hauled it in and pulled it close to his chest before a Cougar pushed him out of bounds.

Having gained enough yardage for a first down and much more, they moved the chains. We all jogged to the new line of scrimmage as the crowd screamed and cheered. I was exhausted as the defense wore me down and kept an eye on the clock.

The advantage of a home game was how quickly I could climb into bed and pass the hell out. The adrenaline that had raced through my veins on the first play had dimmed and I was crashing hard.

We all stood as Torin looked to the sideline, making sense of the hand gestures for the next play.

"I heard you take it in the ass."

The words caught me off guard and my head jerked to the side, not surprised the comment had come from the guy I'd had the displeasure of blocking all day.

Two guys on his team snickered, but I wasn't ashamed of my sexuality. I'd come out before arriving freshman year and honestly didn't give a shit if this guy had a problem with it.

"I'm more of a top," I said with a neutral tone.

His expression switched to confusion, and it was my turn to smirk. He mumbled under his breath. I couldn't make out the exact words, but it wasn't too difficult to catch the gist. And it wasn't anything I hadn't heard on the field before when a player was trying to piss me off into making a mistake.

This time when Torin yelled "Set" and we all dropped, he wasn't at my back. Instead he was farther back, and I knew I needed to shotgun the ball perfectly. We'd done this so many times over the last four years of college, it was second nature. He lifted his leg twice, signaling the snap count so I readied myself.

"Do you give it to the QB?"

The snide comment came at the same moment Torin clapped twice, signaling for the ball. The second I released the ball, I knew I'd fucked up, but there was no time to check the damage. Not when an almost three hundred pound defense player was in my face. I cursed as I took his weight.

It didn't last long before the whistle blew. I turned and my eyes immediately homed in on Torin who was sprawled out on his ass and glaring to his left where a mountain of uniforms piled on top of each other, both teams refusing to budge.

I recognized the aftermath of a fumble and it was my fault. The urge to punch the player who'd thrown me off my game was strong. As many comments that'd been thrown at me about being bisexual, no one had ever connected them with Torin. Besides the one kiss we'd shared back in high school, Torin had never been with a guy. The Cougar was goading me and I fell for it.

Torin accepted my hand and allowed me to pull him up.

"I'm sorry, T."

He wiped his hands on his towel that hung from his uniform. "What happened?"

I hesitated because the game was still going and he couldn't afford the distraction. "Nothing, I fucked up. It won't happen again."

He appeared skeptical with his brows furrowed, but when the turnover was confirmed we had no choice but to leave the field as the other team celebrated and took possession of the football.

Our head coach, Coach Sanders, narrowed his brown eyes at me in a way that promised repercussions. It may have been a mistake, but it was unnecessary and a costly one. I couldn't blame him.

"Sorry, Coach." I pulled off my black and gold helmet and headed straight for the bench where I plopped down and hung my head. How could I let that happen? I was so close to being ready to declare myself eligible for the draft and I made such a big error? I imagined what everyone sitting at home watching the game on TV were saying about me right then. No doubt angry comments were already flooding social media. *Well, that play should make the highlight reel and not in a good way.*

Despite the time of year, I was roasting in my gear, so when a woman approached me and held a bottle up and squirted a sports drink into my mouth, I guzzled as much as she allowed.

"Thanks," I said distractedly.

Torin took a seat beside me, knocking his knee into mine to gain my attention. "Want to tell me the truth now?"

His helmet hung from his fingertips and he ran his other hand through his blond mop of hair. His gaze was too intense so I dropped mine to my cleats. "Nah, it's not a big deal. I mean it is because of what happened, but he caught me off guard with something he said."

He hummed but didn't have time to badger me for more information before the offensive coordinator sat on his opposite side and began to go over plays. I leaned my head back against the railing.

A few more plays like that and my shot at the NFL would be slim. That would be a damn shame because my stats, Torin's too, were good. Better than good and I'd worked hard for them.

"Hey, Rush," Nash said as he propped a grass-stained cleat on the bench. His teeth shined bright against his smooth light brown skin. Though he was smiling, he had to be pissed after making that beauty of a catch only for me to mess up.

I rubbed my hand down my face and groaned.

He chuckled. "Relax, man. I'm not over here to give you shit. But you seem off. Everything all right?"

"Why do you ask?" I squinted because the sun was behind him.

"You look tired." He turned around and sat next to me.

A laugh clawed up my throat. "Why do people always tell you when you look tired? It's like a rule you don't say that."

"Maybe. But we're friends, so I can be honest." Always direct, Nash didn't bother to apologize.

"Well, thanks for that." I glanced around for prying eyes but everyone was focused on the game. I lowered my voice.

"That prick said something and caught me off guard. My fault."

Nash's brows furrowed and he balled his fist at his side. Everyone knew I was bisexual and it was common knowledge I was taunted regularly. It just usually didn't bother me. "What'd he say?"

His midnight black hair was cropped short and his unique yellow-green eyes were enhanced by his dark coloring. Nash was sexy—but unfortunately he knew it and used it to his advantage. He drove both women and men crazy on a level equal to Torin. Luckily, I was immune to Nash's charm.

Nash was also open about his sexuality. He knew what it was like to be bisexual among athletes that used it against him and had been on the receiving end of the same endless trash talk. It was tiresome.

"The usual, but—"

Torin knocked his knee against mine with more force this time and leaned into my space. "Someone said something to you? What's going on?"

His blue eyes bored into mine, encouraging me to tell him what was going on.

"We'll talk after," I promised.

He studied me for a few uncomfortable beats. "Fine, but you have to tell me everything."

We both turned our attention to the big screen just as one of the Cougars' receivers caught a perfectly thrown spiral ball straight into the end zone.

I cost us the game.

FOUR

TORIN

THE CAB of Rush's truck, which still carried that new car smell, was quiet as we rode back to our apartment a few miles from campus. Sometimes I missed the rust bucket he'd gotten rid of months ago and memories of his old truck and our high school days crept up on me. Today they were stronger.

"How much trouble do you think I'm in?" Rush's voice was deep and rough, fitting for his large stature. And though he was grinning, it was a mask I saw through. He was upset with himself and I didn't know how to fix it.

"We just need to give Coach time to calm down. It'll be fine." I held the button down to recline the seat and got comfortable. "You said you'd explain what happened."

His smile dropped into a frown. "You could've gotten hurt."

Though I knew he was redirecting the conversation, he seemed bothered by it more than whatever was said to him. I sighed and turned my head to face him. Without product, my messy hair fell across my forehead. "We play football. We're both likely going to get hurt at some point. It wouldn't even be the first time."

His lips thinned and his whole body grew rigid. "That would've been my fault."

Placing my hand on his thigh, I massaged the giant muscle through the black athletic shorts he'd paired with a black sleeveless t-shirt. It always calmed him down when he was stressed or upset. "It's fine. I'm good. You're good. *We* are good." I stopped rubbing but kept my hand in place.

He cut his eyes over to me and then back to the road. Once. Twice.

"Stop, blaming yourself," I growled while studying his profile.

Rush was sexy and rugged with his straight nose, full lips I'd tasted once and a sharp jaw covered in scruff no matter how many times he shaved.

He exhaled long and hard, sinking down in his seat and only then did I realize how tense he'd been.

"I'll try." He ran his fingers over his buzzed dark hair and when I kept staring, he rolled his eyes. "Yes, sir,"

"Oh, I like where this is going," I purred and pulled my hand back into my lap.

"Never gonna happen." He laughed as he pulled the big black beast of a truck into the apartment complex, circling the parking lot before slowing in front of our building and claimed the spot next to my red Jeep.

Before he shut off the engine, I reached over and clasped his arm. "Promise you'll let this go and move on."

He stared at me, biting his bottom lip. Slowly he nodded. "Fine, yes."

"Promise," I repeated.

"Yes, I promise. Jeez." His amused tone didn't match the annoyed words and my lips twitched.

Satisfied, I released him. He shut off the engine, and though the truck had a lift kit, we only had to simply step out.

Rush was a big guy, dwarfing my tall frame. Unlike many centers, he was a solid wall of muscle. Steady heavy workouts had given me a build I was proud of, but Rush was in a league of his own and had gotten even bigger over four seasons as a Saint. I didn't even think he was aware of the effect he had on people around him. He was magnetic and his presence demanded attention.

Well, he had mine.

After we'd completed the required year of on-campus housing, Rush and I had found this place and it became our home over the last three years.

Climbing the stairs up to our third floor unit was rough after such an intense game, and our bags were quickly ditched in our rooms. We collapsed on opposite ends of the oversized gray fabric couch we'd inherited from the previous occupants. I reached for the remote on the second-hand coffee table and clicked the power button. Highlights of the game filled the flat screen TV.

As if the universe was picking at an already sore subject, Rush and I appeared on screen as the camera zoomed in and the announcers speculated on what had gone wrong and what this loss meant for our season. His posture stiffened, and I huffed out an annoyed breath before quickly changing the channel.

"It's not that big of a deal." Shaking my head, I kicked off my running shoes before sinking into the cushion. I tilted my head back and closed my eyes. "I know it's Saturday and this is pathetic, but I think I'm too tired to do anything other than sleep."

"I'm exhausted and barely holding my eyes open, so

don't feel too bad." The thumps of his shoes hitting the ground somewhere next to mine accompanied Rush's words.

"Good, then I don't have to move." I stretched out across the comfortably worn cushions at my back, using Rush's lap as a rest for my legs, and crossed my arms over my chest.

He chuckled and tapped my legs. "If we're going to sleep, let me up."

Grumbling, I pulled my legs back long enough for him to stand before sprawling back out.

The apartment was small and bare of any hallways, so I tracked Rush's movements as he disappeared into his room. The sounds of fabric rustling as it was removed were followed by a yawn, triggering my own. When he reappeared, he wore only his boxer briefs and headed for the kitchen that was separated from the living room by a small island. He opened the refrigerator, reached in and grabbed a bottle of water.

Rush had always had a nice butt, firm and round, and I took a moment to ogle him as he tipped his head back and took a drink. I'd been tempted a time or two to grab onto it, just to see what he'd do. He'd lost control once before. But in four years not once had he showed any true interest.

He glanced at me. "I don't know how you do that. I can't sleep on the couch much less fully dressed like that."

"I'm too tired to change or move." I complained again and grinned when Rush made his way over. His powerful thighs stretched the navy material to near bursting and I couldn't help but notice his large bulge. I bit my lip as he came close enough all I had to do was reach out and feel him. Would he welcome the touch? Or would he keep pretending he didn't want me?

He set his water on the table and then latched onto my

hands, pulling me into a sitting position before he grabbed the hem of my shirt and jerked the long-sleeved white shirt over my head. Efficient, I thought with a small amount of disappointment.

"Thank you." I stretched and yawned again, hoping his gaze would at least wander. It didn't.

"You're welcome." He rolled his eyes as if he knew exactly what I was up to. He probably did.

After our first, and only, kiss, I'd been excited and ready for the possibilities. I'd been fairly certain he was attracted to me and it had taken me months to build the courage to approach him. It hadn't gone according to my original plan but when he'd kissed me back everything clicked into place. For me at least.

Then the next morning happened. The news about his uncle had rocked his world and I recognized his need for space. So I'd been there in the only way I knew how. As his best friend.

Four years later and I was still trying to accept that what had sparked between us that night was dead. But I just didn't believe it. I couldn't. I'd slowly driven myself crazy. I needed to know if I was alone in my struggle to remain friend-zoned. My sigh was loud.

Rush picked up his water from the table. "What now?"

"I'm still dressed." I gestured to the gray and black training pants.

He snorted but his gaze dipped to my lower half. "You're on your own there, buddy."

Knowing what was underneath, I stood and yanked down my pants, leaving me completely naked.

A strangled sound came from Rush's throat and he coughed into his hand. "Don't sit your bare ass on the couch."

When I glanced at him, he eyes were trained on the wall over my head, his expression blank.

"Fine."

He stood stiff as a board as I strode to my bedroom, leaving my "bare ass" on display.

Rush's whispered curse met my ears just before his door shut a little harder than necessary. I counted it as a win.

My room was dark at the late hour as I climbed into bed. After my head hit the pillow and I curled on my side. Then I thought about the game and realized he'd never told me what the guy had said. There was no way I was getting out of bed and with the way he'd slammed his door, I didn't think it wise to go knocking. So I picked up my phone and pulled up our messages.

"You never told me what that guy said to you that threw you off so bad."

The dots bounced around as he typed before going away. Then it happened again. After the fourth time, I wondered if he'd answer at all so I set my phone on my nightstand and had almost drifted off when my phone lit up and buzzed. I reached out so quickly, I nearly knocked it to the floor. Pulling up his response, my mouth fell open.

"He asked me if I fucked you."

FIVE

TORIN

"DON'T FORGET." Professor Basset did his best to speak loud enough to be heard over the crowded stadium style lecture room. "Assignments are due tomorrow before you leave for break. No exceptions."

We'd spent Sunday finishing ours and had already emailed them, but as I glanced around, I noted some panicked expressions and was glad we'd knocked them out.

Students stood, gathering their things and chatting with friends. Everyone was excited for Thanksgiving break and going home to visit family. One more day of classes and then most of the student body would vacate the campus. Unless you were an athlete. The Saints' football team would be on a bus Thanksgiving Day taking the long trip to Northern Oklahoma to play against the Tigers Friday.

Since we couldn't make it home for the holiday, the last three years, Rush and I created a new tradition. We celebrated the day after the game so we could enjoy the entire weekend back home.

At my side, Rush slid his laptop into his bag before slipping it onto his shoulder, something I'd already done. He was moving slow, and it was obvious he was procrastinating on purpose.

"Practice still starts at the same time, even if you move at the speed of a turtle." I bumped his arm with mine before I turned and led us down the rows of seats.

"Doesn't mean I plan to skip my way there." His grumpy tone made me smile. He continued his lazy pace as he followed me down the aisle toward the exit.

I chuckled and after hesitating a moment, he joined in.

"It'll be fine."

He scoffed. "I know, but you know how Coach is. He'll make the whole team pay for my mistake. Makes me feel like shit."

"We've all been punished as a team for less." I narrowed my eyes at him over my shoulder. "And you promised you'd let it go."

"I know." He reached over me to push open the door and held it as I passed under his arm. I marveled again at his size.

The weather was perfect in the upper sixties and the sun warmed my face as we walked down the sidewalk. I'd worn jeans and a light jacket because of the chill that morning but I pulled it off on our way.

Nash caught up to us and sidled up next to me. He had a cherry sucker in his mouth, an accessory he was rarely without. He pulled it out as he turned to keep pace with me.

"You and Rush ready to face Coach?" His question was whispered for my ears only, but Rush must have heard it anyway.

"I'm going to run to the truck and grab our gear." He stalked off quicker than I could reply.

"Thanks." I glared at Nash. "He already thinks he may have cost us our chance of making the playoffs."

And he thinks he allowed me to get hurt because an asshole asked if we were fucking.

We'd taken the day before to rest, but practice resumed in just over an hour. Maybe Coach had cooled off and ready to move on. Not likely.

Nash held his hands up, palms out as he matched my steps. "Don't shoot the messenger. I had no idea he was so worked up over it." He frowned. "I guess it's never been him Coach has been pissed at."

"Does it matter who Coach is mad at? Punish one, punish us all."

"Point taken." Nash adjusted the strap on his shoulder and popped his sucker back in his mouth.

Out in the quad, we met up with Bishop and Shaw. Both stood under a tree, resembling supermodels instead of two of the roughest football players on the team. Shaw was light on his feet, fast as hell and could make impossible plays. Bishop was a safety on defense. If a runner was lucky enough to make it past our defensive line, they went up against the dark prince himself. At least that's how I thought of him.

Shaw had blond hair and emerald green eyes. Bishop's hair was the deepest black with equally dark eyes. Shaw attended Sugar Land on a football scholarship and Bishop's dad had more money than heart. Where Shaw was outgoing and friendly, Bishop made you want to keep your distance. The only similarity was their reputations on the field. They, along with Nash, were all juniors and still had another year with the Saints.

I pulled my phone from my pocket and glanced at the

time. We would be late if we didn't get moving and I was ready to be done with it. Rush had taken his sweet time again.

"Where's Rush?" I asked absently as I slapped palms with Bishop and Shaw.

Bishop said nothing, a normal response, but Shaw's gaze focused over my shoulder. "He's headed this way."

"Was starting to think he'd taken his truck and run." I pivoted around as the guys chuckled behind me.

Glancing at my invisible watch, I gave Rush a quirky grin as he approached.

He cracked a reluctant smile and handed me my bag. "Let's get this shit over with."

The campus was lucky enough to have a completely updated indoor athletic facility that included a full-size field and separate weight room. Once we stepped through the glass doors, we headed straight for the locker room to dress out in our practice uniforms.

"Unless we want to give him another reason to make today difficult, we better hurry," I muttered to Rush. The others were already filing out as I finished lacing my cleats.

"We? I'm done and waiting on you. Who's the one being slow now?" Rush lifted one brow and grinned.

When I glared at him, he winked. "In a better mood, are we?"

He shrugged. "Nothing I can do about it. I'm here, so let's do this."

A slow smile stretched across my face as I followed him out. We'd barely stepped one foot onto the indoor practice field before Coach Sanders stomped in our direction.

"Here we go," I warned as Rush whistled under his breath.

"Hopkins and Jaggers, let's go!" Coach barked.

We met him halfway before he redirected us to an unused side of the field. Rush and I exchanged confused glances, but knew better than to question him.

"Here." Coach smacked a football into Rush's hands. "I'm not interested in excuses because it doesn't matter what happened. What matters is that you handle it. You want to play in the NFL, Jaggers?"

"I do," Rush confirmed and tucked the ball under one arm.

"Then you better make sure it doesn't happen again." He narrowed his eyes. "Now, you two will stretch it out and then practice snaps today."

"The entire time?" I asked in shock.

"For as long as I say. You got a problem with that, Hopkins?" Coach challenged and took a step toward me.

Again I traded a look with Rush. Coach had lost his mind.

"No, sir," I replied although I thought the exercise was useless. But I couldn't tell him the truth about what had screwed up that play.

"Good." He leveled a look at both me and Rush that dared us to question him again before leaving us.

Like Rush, I'd never been singled out or on the receiving end of his wrath before. I couldn't say I was a fan. As much of a waste I considered this practice, it was Coach's call. I dropped to the ground, Rush claimed the space in front of me and we stretched.

"Well this should be fun," Rush grumbled with one long leg out to the side as he gripped the toe of his cleat.

I pretended to pout. "Working with me is such a hardship?"

"Shut up." He rolled his eyes. "No, it just seems pointless."

My brows furrowed. "My guess is that he knows the exercise itself is pointless and to make sure we don't do it again. This is our punishment. Instead of working us to death, he's going to bore us to death."

"Whatever you say." He switched to the other leg.

We stretched in silence for several more minutes before I climbed to my feet. I picked up the ball and held it out to him. "Now bend over."

He scowled but stood and snatched the ball from my hands. "That's not how I roll. You'd be bent over."

The moan that crawled up my throat nearly slipped free and my ass clenched as I wondered exactly what that would feel like. I could only imagine since I'd never had sex with a guy before, but my imagination was vivid where Rush was concerned.

"You wish," I croaked.

He crouched in position several feet in front of me, his perfect ass lifted for my viewing pleasure. "Set."

I called for the ball and the exchange was smooth like the million other times we'd done it. As if in a real game, I took several steps back pretending to look for a receiver.

"This is so stupid," Rush was quick to say once he stood.

I agreed, but Coach was just crazy enough to bench our asses if we argued.

"No point in complaining, big man. Now bend back over."

He pointed at me. "You're asking for it."

"You want it," I teased and his nostrils flared, giving me pause. He looked somewhere between pissed off and turned on.

With one more pointed look, he got back into position.

After fifteen minutes of the same thing over and over, Coach Sanders's voice interrupted us. "That's enough. Get out here and do it with the team."

Apparently, we'd been observed. I thought we'd gotten off, but then he lined the whole team up and made us practice snap after snap until most of the team was shooting us glares.

SIX

RUSH

"FIVE MORE!" Coach's voice echoed in the weight room.

"Thank fuck," Torin gritted between his teeth as he pushed the bar up for the last time. My fingers hovered just beneath as I spotted him until he placed it securely back into the bracket. He sat up slowly, shaking out his arms. Sweat ran down his temple and his tan skin flushed red from exertion. "Will you hand me my drink?"

I bent down, grabbed the bottle and handed it to him. My gaze stayed glued to the way his throat moved as he swallowed and moaned in appreciation. Metal clanged as one by one my teammates finished with weight training, breaking the trance.

"Thanks." He twisted the lid back on.

Muttering a curse, I set about putting the weights away. When Torin tried to help, I waved him off. "Go ahead. I'll be there in a minute."

His lips pursed as he watched me grab another weight, but eventually left me alone. My muscles ached in the best way from the set I'd finished before switching positions with Torin, but I welcomed the burn. Lifting was therapy, distracting me from life's problems. *Torin was not a problem.*

I was last to the locker room and guys were already getting ready to leave, including Torin. After grabbing my small caddy from my locker, I stripped down and slipped beneath the warm spray. With efficient movements I washed, wanting nothing more than to be back at the apartment, lounging and recovering.

After I dried off, I jammed my legs back into shorts and tugged on my shirt. The locker room had emptied, but I found Torin waiting just outside the door. Dressed in jeans and a hooded sweatshirt, he leaned against the wall with his hands in his pockets.

His gaze traveled over me, head to toe, and he shook his head. "I'll never understand how the cold doesn't affect you."

My lip twitched as I fought a smile. "I'll never understand why you always look like you'll freeze if every inch of you isn't bundled up."

He chuckled as we both adjusted our bags over our shoulder and made our way outside. The weather was giving me whiplash. Only a few hours had passed but as we approached late afternoon, it was noticeably colder.

Torin tucked his hands farther into his pockets as we hurried back to my truck and climbed in the roomy cab. Rarely did we take Torin's Jeep, and that suited my big ass just fine.

"You think Coach is satisfied now?" I asked as I started the truck.

Torin pulled his seatbelt down and clicked it into place and chuckled. "I'm not sure that man is ever satisfied."

I cranked the heater on high for Torin. "Truth."

Coach Sanders wasn't known for a winning personality,

but he trained more NFL first-round picks than any other current head coach. We didn't have to like his style, but we couldn't argue with the results.

I pulled out of the space and headed for the highway, making the short trip back to our place. As we ascended the stairs, Torin led the way and my gaze strayed down to his tight, round ass. He'd been joking around a lot about sexual things and I found my thoughts drifting to things it shouldn't. Like how biteable his ass looked in those jeans. He had me confused but how did I approach the subject with him? *T, I'm going to need you to stop acting like you want to fuck because I'm at my breaking point.* My nose scrunched. *Okay, maybe not the best way to handle it.*

His keys jingled before the door swung open and we both dropped our practice bags by the front door, knowing we'd need to take them to the laundry soon.

A muscle in my back started to spasm and I winced.

Torin's gaze cut to mine. "What's wrong?"

I tilted my head from side to side, stretching the muscles that had cramped from lifting. "Muscles are cramping," I said and twisted my torso, trying to relieve the pain.

"Oh, why didn't you say something?" he asked and then dragged me by the hand to the couch. When I sat, he pushed me forward and climbed behind me. Torin straddled my body, and then his knuckles sank into the knotted muscles of my back. I groaned as he worked on a stubborn area. His hands moved to my shoulders, kneading and soothing the tension.

I may not have admitted the full truth of what was wrong, but hadn't lied about the aches and pains. My neck was treated next and his touch softened. The firm yet gentle massage left me boneless.

My chest ached like it did every time Torin showed me

how much he cared. It was bittersweet because, even though we loved each other, what would happen when he met someone and fell *in* love and that devotion shifted to them? Visions of a future heartbreak distressed me when I allowed my mind to wander, so I struggled to focus. He'd always be my best friend and nothing had to change.

"Feel good?" he whispered in my ear.

Incapable of words, I groaned in response and didn't protest as he ran a finger down my spine, stopping on my lower back. Pressing deep, he dug into my flesh. His touch drifted to my sides and then inched around toward my front. The closer he moved toward my cock, the harder it grew until I sported a raging hard-on.

Torin wasn't immune. His swollen shaft pressed flush against my back. A gasp ripped free from my throat and I shifted my hips.

"Fucking hell," he rasped.

It shocked me back to reality and I jerked forward.

Startled, he removed his hands from my body. "Whoa."

"Sorry," I mumbled as I stood. "I think I better get some sleep."

Torin's gaze locked with mine before he gave a solid nod. "Yeah, that sounds like a good idea."

"Thanks for your help with the... for the..." I paused. "Good night."

SEVEN

TORIN

"WHY ARE YOU STARING?" Rush asked from the driver's seat of his truck as we drove to meet up with Nash, Shaw and Bishop for lunch.

My face heated and I knew my cheeks were blooming red. Luckily, he kept his eyes on the road. I'd been thinking about last night and hadn't realized I'd been openly gawking.

Neither of us had addressed the night before. The rejection stung, though I should have expected it. When he'd responded the way he had, I hadn't been thinking straight. He'd wanted more but wouldn't let himself have it. It was beyond frustrating.

I couldn't tell him I was imaging how the night could have gone. After we'd come so close to crossing the line, I didn't think he was ready to hear it, so I went with the second thing that caught my attention.

"Shorts." I flicked a finger toward his lower half. The day before had been in the upper sixties but today we hovered at forty-five degrees. That was heavy jacket weather in my opinion. I tugged the sleeves down of my gray hooded sweater over my hands and shivered

"How long have we known each other?" He gave me a slow blink as he reached over and turned up the heat.

I scoffed. "And yet it never ceases to amaze me."

He pulled into the curbside parking space in front of the sandwich shop. We stepped out of the truck and headed for the door. Our table was impossible to miss with three guys towering over the other customers even while seated.

I wound through the clusters of tables, accidentally bumping into a few chairs with Rush behind me until I reached our group. We claimed two of the six chairs on one side. Bishop and Shaw sat next to each other to our left and Nash occupied the two remaining seats with his feet kicked up on one.

"Well, practice sucked yesterday," Shaw greeted us.

Nash yanked his sucker out of his mouth and pointed it at Shaw. "Don't start."

"What?" Shaw shrugged and pushed a messy strand of light blond hair behind his ear. "It did. I'd rather be falling on my ass tired than bored for an hour while you two toss the ball back and forth. That was brutal."

"Dramatic much." Nash rolled his eyes.

Bishop said nothing as usual and sat with his back against the wall. The hood of his black jacket was pulled over his dark hair, leaving his face shadowed. His piercing dark eyes seemed to see more than everyone else. Intense fucker made me squirm sometimes just looking at him.

"Sorry, guys," Rush apologized and glanced around the shop. "Did y'all already order? I'm starving."

He didn't seem all that bothered and I grinned. It was about time he let it go, so I flipped off Shaw behind Rush's back.

"We already ordered." He returned the gesture with a shit-eating grin. "We weren't going to wait on you jackasses. Who knew when y'all would crawl out of bed after—"

"The fuck, Shaw? Shut up." Bishop's raspy voice cut off whatever Shaw was going on about.

When Shaw fell silent, I studied them together. Bishop went back to brooding and Shaw held his hands up. "Damn, I was just joking."

Nash shook his head. "You two give me a headache." As if to further his point, he rubbed his temples.

As we waited for the waitress, I couldn't help but glance between Shaw and Bishop. Like Rush and I, they were together a lot, but their relationship was clear as mud.

My stomach growled just as a woman with a short blond bob and wearing a black apron approached our table while balancing three drinks on a tray. She stopped at the side of our table and set them in front of the other guys.

"They said two more were coming." Her attention shifted from me to Rush as she lifted a small notepad from the pouch on her uniform. "Do you boys know what you want?"

"Two waters, lemon on the side. Two cheeseburgers with everything on them and a plate of fries," Rush responded, and I nodded in confirmation.

"Extra pickles," I added.

She wrote the order and stuck the pen behind her ear. "Your drinks will be right out."

When she was beyond ear shot, Nash leaned his elbows on the table. "So, I heard Coach is leaving next year."

"Really? Where did you hear that?" Rush sounded skeptical, and I didn't blame him.

Nash shrugged. "I might have overheard the assistant coach having a conversation about it."

"No way would Sugar Land fire him," Shaw insisted.

Nash hummed around his straw as he took a sip. "He may be an asshole, but no, they wouldn't. From what I understood, he got a better offer we can't match or something."

I leaned back in my chair. "Well, lucky for you guys next year then."

"So?" Nash said, switching topics before I could wrap my head around the first conversation. "Do you think we have a shot at making the playoffs? I think we might."

"We've only had the one loss. So yeah, I think we have a chance."

He held his hand up and I reached over to high-five him.

"You heard it, people! The captain says we are taking the Saints to the playoffs!" Nash's voice rose so the whole place could hear him.

A few hoots in the restaurant followed his loud comment.

"Go Saints!" one particular male fan shouted and a few people laughed.

Not exactly what'd I'd said, but close enough. I glanced at Rush and shared a grin. This was all we'd ever wanted growing up. We'd dreamed of playing in the NFL the first time we threw a ball around. But while his goal was still to play pro ball, my interests had turned to the strategic side of the game. Every time one coordinator set me down to go over the plays, I was engrossed in the mental creativity and challenge of designing new plays, scoping out next week's opponent, and choosing the right players to execute the strategy.

I'd learned that I really enjoyed the analytical part of the game and was ready to run my own business and face my own challenges. There was something satisfying about the thought of making something from nothing. Using my ideas, I could build from the ground up. But I couldn't shake football from my system completely. My plan was to start an online shop specializing in sporting goods, and the dream was to grow it into a prosperous franchise.

My stomach sank just like it did every time I thought about it. We were in our last year of college and with any luck, Rush was on track to being drafted. There was no telling which team would choose him or where he'd end up. Would it be weird if I moved to stay close to him? After all, I could start an online business anywhere.

It was something I knew we both wondered about but avoided the topic.

"Anyway, Bishop's dad is throwing a party at his new club in Dallas on Saturday night. He wants us to come celebrate our expected win." Shaw chuckled.

"And if we don't win?" Rush asked just as the woman showed up with all five orders, setting the plates down in front of us.

I smirked at Shaw when he scowled at my plate and then me. He should have waited, I thought.

I snatched the ketchup and squirted a small mountain onto our full plate of fries.

"Then I guess we drink our troubles away," Shaw recovered and suggested.

My attention shifted to Bishop who appeared content drinking a milkshake. He didn't seem to have anything to add as he sat there silently with his gaze on Shaw.

"We're heading to Riverside for the weekend as soon as we get back, so we won't be able to make it this time," I replied and looked to Rush.

"Definitely next time." He glanced at his watch. "But we need to leave. We have class in thirty minutes."

"Shit, time flew fast," I said. And then we were stuffing our faces.

EIGHT

RUSH

AFTER OUR LAST class that day and saying goodbye to many of the students who were leaving campus for break, we'd made it to practice. We watched film for an hour before Coach had us on the outside field, running through offensive plays.

"I'm feeling good about this one," Beau, our defense captain said, narrowing his eyes across from me. "Torin's going down."

I scoffed. "Not fucking likely."

He chuckled and I smirked as we squatted into position.

Coach Sanders yelled a play to Torin and then addressed the team, "Once more and then hit the showers."

"Ready!" Torin yelled as our line crouched, facing our own defense linemen. "Set."

The second he called for the ball, I shot it through my legs and locked up with Beau. He rivaled me in size, but had more gut. Though he was strong and they could only touch Torin, not tackle him, I put my all into it and he hadn't made it by me yet.

"Good!" Coach clapped and we all relaxed. "I expect this to be how this weekend's game is played."

The rest of the coaching staff walked out onto the field, talking to individuals about things they'd seen and most likely some minor adjustments they wanted to make. Coach Sanders approached me so I released my chin strap and removed my helmet. Torin appeared at my side like my guardian angel. A snort escaped me when I caught sight of his blond hair sticking up in all directions, even worse than usual. In return an elbow met my ribs.

"Ouch," I muttered and held my hand over my side.

"Stop being a baby," Torin volleyed back with a wink.

"You two look good out there. I take it whatever was on your minds has been resolved?" Coach asked, his mouth set in a firm line.

"Yes, sir." I couldn't tell him it had been a taunt that had thrown me off so bad. Comments meant to shake the other team were to be expected. We were taught to be ready for it, disciplined to overlook it. That didn't always work.

Coach nodded once and then continued on, dismissing us.

"Speaking of which, what are we doing tonight?" Torin asked as I followed him inside toward the locker room.

"Is this a trick question?" I yawned.

Torin glanced over his shoulder and waggled his brows. "Want to get crazy and rent a movie?"

"I don't know. Seems a little wild and I'm tired." He stopped abruptly, making me knock into him. "What are you doing?"

"You're not avoiding me are you because of last night, are you?" His tone held a note of accusation.

"Relax." I placed my hand on his shoulder and gave a

light squeeze. "I was joking. We can rent a movie or whatever. I just want to be home."

He stood for a moment longer and audibly exhaled. "Good."

We stepped into the spacious room, our teammates spread throughout in various states of their after practice routine. The room hummed with smack talk and general chaos like it always did when the two sides played against each other, both sides swearing they were better.

As voices rose, Torin and I stripped down and tied towels around our waists and gathered our products from our lockers.

"Good thing we play for the same side," Torin said as we cranked on individual shower heads and stripped off our towels.

I chuckled and stepped beneath the spray and dug through my caddy for my bar soap. "It would be weird playing against each other."

"Right?" he mused as the sound of his soap lid cracked open and then snapped closed beside me. "We have always done everything together."

"Not *everything*." I froze with my hand lathered in soap against my chest. I hadn't meant to say that out loud.

The surrounding buzz of chatter disappeared and my head swam. Reluctantly, I cut my eyes toward Torin. He stood still and his gaze burned a hole through my side.

"We could always change that. You bending over for me all the time—it's not like I haven't thought about it."

His words set my skin on fire and his cheeky tone made me want to spank his ass. My dick perked up and I quickly scanned the room. Most everyone had left but a few stragglers remained by the lockers. Torin and I were alone in the showers.

"Yeah?" I attempted to match his tone but failed when my voice cracked.

He picked up where he left off, nonchalantly soaping his body. But I knew he was doing this shit on purpose. Torin wanted a reaction, was testing my limits. He wrapped his soapy hand around his hard cock and stroked once. He bit his lip and met my stare. "Sure. You have a nice ass. I'd totally fuck it."

He barely managed the last word before I had his back pressed against the wall. Gripping him around the waist with one arm, the other braced against the tiles. "Let's get one thing straight, T. I'd fuck *you* and I'd fuck you hard. I'd slip inside your tight ass as you screamed my name and begged me for more."

He gasped and shifted his hips, rocking his hard cock against mine. "Rush," he moaned from deep in his throat.

I listened for anyone around, but all was quiet. A quick glance behind me confirmed we were alone, and then I dipped my head next to his ear. "I'd stretch you around my cock, filling you over and over until you came and dragged every drop of my come into your hot hole."

He squirmed as he tilted his head back, exposing his neck. "Please touch me."

I removed my hand from his waist and stood upright so I could touch more of him. Starting with his sides, I caressed his body, running my short nails against his flushed skin. When I met the slight flare of his hips, I circled my hands around to his muscular cheeks and grabbed a handful of each.

The smooth column of his throat was more than I could resist. I dragged my tongue up the pulsing vein and whispered in his ear, "I am touching you."

"More," he hissed and my cock pulsed.

I spread him, continuing to massage his cheeks as they softened beneath my hands.

Inching my fingers toward his crease, I watched for any signs of hesitancy. As the first touch of my finger against his entrance, he cried out and clawed at the back of my neck, pulling me down. Just as I was about to kiss him, a loud bang echoed off the walls, causing us both to jump and jerk away from each other. I scanned the room, searching for the cause of the sound, and saw a man from the cleanup crew pulling a metal cart into the locker room.

I cleared my throat, catching the employee's attention. After a quick apology he exited and I faced Torin again.

The moment had been interrupted, but heat blazed in his cobalt-blue eyes, unconcealed and bare. I had so many questions. "Is this a bad idea?"

"It would be a great idea if you would stop fighting it." Frustration bled into his tone as he stepped away and grabbed his towel on his way out of the shower.

"What do you mean?" I followed behind him and refastened my towel.

He scrubbed his hands over his face. "Let's go home. We don't need to do this here."

My cock was still hard, which made getting dressed uncomfortable. I attempted to ignore that Torin wasn't in much better shape.

The ride back to the apartment was painfully quiet. Neither of us had spoken a word since leaving the campus parking lot and worry set in.

"Should we talk about it?" I finally asked and cut my eyes to him before glancing back to the road. "I won't lie, T, I'm a little confused."

He released a deep breath, his posture relaxing. "I'm not sure what was so confusing about that."

My eyes stayed on his stoic expression. "Everything. Lately you've been different. What's going on?"

"Good different or bad different?" His tone was laced with wariness.

I paused and thought of everything. "I don't know."

Torin nodded and with a tight smile glanced at me. "Let me know when you figure it out then."

NINE
RUSH

TORIN WAS STILL ASLEEP when I left the apartment, just as the sun peeked over the horizon. Since class was out, our busy schedule relaxed some. Attempting to clear my head, I set off for the trail behind the complex as his words from the day before played over and over like a broken record.

"Let me know when you figure it out then."

The air was crisp and the pink sky gradually turned to a bright, clear blue. I ran for miles along the wooded path lined with huge oak trees until my legs burned and my clothes were soaked through before I returned home with no more clarity than when I'd left.

Torin sat on the couch, outfitted for conditioning, and finishing a protein shake. He didn't spare me a glance when I walked through the door, and I stood there letting the awkwardness fester.

"I'm going to grab a shower and we can go," I finally said.

"Ready when you are." He gave a humorless chuckle. "Well, ain't that the truth?"

After a short cool shower, I dressed and grabbed everything, including Torin's gear. I tossed the straps over my shoulder and he followed me from the apartment to the truck.

We drove in silence, but only a few minutes had passed when I cracked. "I hate this."

"Hate what?" He was staring out his window and didn't turn to face me.

"This. You ignoring me. Feeling awkward with you." I gripped the wheel tight. "I don't even know what to do."

"Maybe you should have thought about that before you almost fucked me in the shower." Despite his words, his tone was flat.

"I never would have fucked you in the shower, T. Yes, things got out of control, but I have more respect for you than that. If it went that far, it wouldn't be like that." *Why are we talking about fucking, and why had we been all over each other in the shower? More to the point, why had he reciprocated or instigated it. Had he instigated it?* My head spun.

He turned to me with the saddest expression and it broke my heart. "Look, I hate this too. If I'm wrong, and you're not into me that way, then tell me."

"I think it's obvious I'm attracted to you, T. But we can't just mess around or whatever is happening here. I don't think I could handle that." Maybe if I was honest then we could get back on steady ground, keeping our friendship intact.

He sighed. "I don't mean into me physically. I meant like *be* with me. If not, it might take me some time, but I'm not going anywhere. We'll still be friends. I'm just... hurt."

"I don't understand." My brows furrowed as I glanced from him and back to the road.

His expression twisted with frustration. "I tried to tell you once before. Rush, I've been waiting for you to be ready for four years."

My foot tapped the brake hard and the truck lurched sideways. Without thought, I threw my arm in front of Torin as a shield.

"Maybe we should talk about this once we get parked," I suggested as I sped back up, checking my mirrors and paying extra attention to the road. If I started to contemplate what he'd just said, I was likely to wreck the damn truck.

The minute I found an empty space on campus, I pulled in and parked before facing Torin. "Please explain."

He groaned and tugged on his hair. "That kiss in high school, I thought it was the start of something different between us. But the next day... I kept waiting for the right time to talk, but it never happened."

"You aren't gay." *Brilliant, Rush.*

"No, but what happened yesterday doesn't exactly make me straight either, does it?"

"Why wouldn't you tell me?"

"Tell you what? That I was into you?" His voice shook and he placed his hand on the door handle. "I'm the one who kissed you back then."

"I thought I was an experiment!" My voice rose. "You haven't been with a guy as far as I know since then. And then yesterday, and the massage..."

"And I told you that you didn't get to decide whether I was serious or not! I wasn't looking for a one-time thing, and you weren't a fucking experiment! I also made it clear then and it's still true today that you are the only man I've ever been attracted to physically."

That whole night and day had been a chaotic mix of

confusion and hurt after first, kissing my best friend and then, finding out that my dad was really my uncle. I really didn't remember him saying that. And then, I'd struggled to resist the feelings that tormented me. I'd even thought that I made the right call when Torin had never talked about another guy in four years.

"You've dated other people," I stated, almost accusingly.

He bit his lip and cast his gaze down to his lap. "Only after you did. I hated it."

My stomach knotted with guilt. I hadn't known. How was that possible, and what did he mean I was the only man? I needed clarification. "So you're bisexual?"

"Do you even listen? No, because I'm not attracted to men. Only you!" He was trembling and clenching his fists in sheer exasperation. "If that makes me bisexual, then fine. Does it even matter?"

The hush that fell over the cab of the truck was interrupted by both of our heavy breathing, and the pulse of my racing heart pounded in my ears. I kept my eyes on his, searching his sky-blues, wondering how we came to this moment.

"That doesn't make sense," is what I settled on, which seemed to really piss him off.

He was out of the truck and grabbing his bag, apparently done with the conversation. He slung it over his shoulder and marched off.

I jumped out, reaching for my gear as well. I took off after him. The campus was deserted other than a few athletes all headed in the same direction, toward the athletic building. "Torin," I called, but he didn't stop.

Finally he halted by the door and waited for me. Once I stood beside him, he glanced up, letting me see his pain.

I reached for him but he took a step back. "Don't do this. Give me time to sort my shit. This was a lot to take in."

"Tell me something." He searched my eyes. "Was it ever me for you?"

"What do you mean?" My throat went dry as the truth begged to be set free. It was always him.

He closed his eyes and slowly shook his head. "I'm not playing games. I've been teasing you, I know, but even then, it's not a game. I just want you to want me back."

"T—" I tried, but I was too late. He turned and opened the door before I could think of the right thing to say. But what was the right thing? Confused was far too mild of a word to describe the onslaught of emotions that were coiling through my mind and heart.

Too many teammates were already in the weight room when I entered to be able to talk to Torin, so I started stretching and going through my routine before I loaded my weights. When I was ready to lift, Torin was there ready to spot me. He didn't say a word, but he was there. That had to mean *something*. Maybe I hadn't destroyed us.

We switched places when I finished my set and he never once looked me in the eye. Even though he swore he just needed time to get over it, I wasn't sure I could now. I'd suppressed my feelings for him for so long because I worried I'd lose him. And now it felt like even our friendship was in jeopardy. I needed to get my thoughts in order before I opened my mouth and upset the situation even more.

Torin carried on with the guys like any other day, but I kept to myself. I couldn't hold a normal conversation. I wasn't in the headspace. When the weights were put away, equipment cleaned and the time for practice scheduled for hours later, I decided to waste time watching film. With any luck, it would distract me enough that afterward, I could think clearly.

Torin stepped into my path just as I was about to exit into the hall. "The guys want to go grab some food. Are you coming?"

He surprised me by talking to me at all so I stuttered, "I think I'm going to skip today."

He glanced at me and then the door. With a tight expression he nodded. "See you at practice then."

"Yeah, see you." Swallowing hard, I followed the hallway toward the media room. Empty black plastic chairs were lined in rows in front of large folding tables. A flat screen was perched on a rolling cart that had been locked into place front and center. I tossed my bag onto one of the vacant chairs and dug around for a protein bar and sports drink. Once I'd located them, I plucked the remote from the rolling cart and took a seat in front of the screen.

When my phone buzzed, I silenced it without glancing at the screen. I didn't know what to say or do, afraid that whatever move I made would be the wrong one. Worry settled heavily in my gut. If I acted on whatever was happening between us, I might lose him. If I didn't, I might lose him.

After powering the TV on, I scrolled through the digital files until I located the clip of the Tigers against the number two team last year and hit play.

I studied the movements of the defense, how they fed off each other's energy and the rhythm they seemed comfortable with. As my thoughts returned to Torin, the TV became background noise.

I'd always wanted him, but now that he'd confessed he wanted me too, it would be impossible to press rewind and forget it. So what was stopping me? Why was I struggling to continue walking the line I desperately want to cross with him? Torin was clearly trying to tug me across it. Four years he'd waited? I couldn't wrap my head around it. I closed my eyes tight, imagining moments with him over the last four years. How had I missed it?

Thinking about being with Torin, not just physically, but being able to call him mine, sent a thrill up my spine. It was a huge risk, but it might be my only shot. Would we have been together by now if my trust hadn't been shattered by that secret kept from me by my own parents? Torin had been there throughout the confusion, pieced me together and held me whole. Though I'd long since accepted the situation for what it was and my anger had faded, my trust took longer to heal. But I never doubted Torin. Not for a second.

I was attracted to Torin, inside and out. I craved his company above all others. Would I love to be in a romantic relationship? Without a doubt. And I believed him when he said he reciprocated those feelings. Maybe it was time to try. If I walked away from this, it would haunt me forever. The what-ifs. I had to try, didn't I? Allowing myself to really imagine Torin and me being an 'us' made me smile. I needed to talk to him after practice.

An arm slung around my neck, startling me. Nash smirked as he dropped into the chair beside me. I knew that expression. He was up to no good.

"What?" I asked.

"Missed you at lunch today and you ignored my text." His yellow-green eyes narrowed.

I pulled my phone out of my pocket. There were five missed called and fifteen fucking unread text messages. "I put my phone on silent and forgot."

"That's too bad." He leaned back in the chair. "You missed Torin getting mauled by a fan girl."

I rolled my eyes and glanced back at the game on the screen. "Like that's new."

He removed his arm and twisted his body to sit sideways. "Yep, but crazy thing, Torin and her are going on a date."

My face flushed hot, my stomach rolled and my throat seemed to close as the words sank in.

"No, Torin is not." The smooth voice came from behind me. "She asked for my number and I said no."

I turned and saw him glare at Nash. When I flicked my gaze over to Nash, his eyes danced with mirth as he glanced back and forth between us. "Oops. Maybe I misunderstood. See ya in a few." With a wink, he turned and jogged out of the room.

I stared off after him in confusion. "What the hell was that?"

Torin gathered my things. "Who knows, it's Nash and you're late. Coach sent us for you so you better hurry."

"Shit." I glanced at my phone again. I hadn't paid attention to the time, and I was fifteen minutes late. Only then did I notice Torin was in his practice uniform minus his helmet. Nash had been in his gear too.

We both sprinted to the indoor field, but just before we crossed the threshold, I stopped and turned toward Torin. I couldn't get through practice with something so heavy on my mind.

I inhaled deeply and let it out slowly. "What if I said I wanted to try?"

He crossed his arms. "You may want to clarify that question. Because if I assume it's about us and it's not, then I really won't forgive you."

I cracked a smile and felt my cheeks heat. I felt like I was asking out my first crush, and I guessed that's exactly what I was doing.

A slow smile spread across his face, and he sank his teeth into his bottom lip before he returned the smile. "Really?"

"Hopkins and Jaggers! This isn't play time and why aren't you dressed out?" Coach belted across the room, his voice booming off the walls.

"Really," I whispered before I rushed off for the locker room, leaving Torin to deal with Coach.

———

"HOW KIND of you to join us, Jaggers. To the sideline with Hopkins." Coach scowled.

Torin waited where we'd practiced several times, tossing a football in the air and catching it.

As the rest of the team worked with their respective specialty coaches, I spoke up to Coach. "I thought we served our sentence."

He lifted a brow. "You're done when I'm convinced this week's game will be a win. You couldn't even bother to show up to practice on time. And considering your position, Hopkins is the only one who can practice with you. So if he's not happy, well I suggest you show up on time."

Knowing he wouldn't relent, my mouth set in a firm line. "I won't be late again."

"See that you aren't."

I waited for him to walk off before I headed in Torin's direction.

"Here we go again," Torin muttered and tossed me a ball.

"I think he gets off on making us do this stupid stuff."

"Wouldn't surprise me." He clapped his hands. "Ready!"

I rolled my eyes and turned before bending down into my position

"Speaking of getting off." He let out a low whistle. "There is one benefit to this."

"Torin," I cautioned. His lighthearted chuckle caused me to grin. "Just catch the damn ball."

And he did, over and over until I felt him right behind me. "Maybe we should practice snapping under center."

Straightening, I gave him an incredulous look. "Coach hardly ever calls those plays and I'm not going to screw that up."

"You never know." Torin pursed his lips and shook his head gravely. "I've seen games lost due to fumbles during that exchange. It'd be a shame if that happened."

I eyed him with suspicion. "Fine, but for the record, I think this is stupid."

"Noted," he said with a crooked grin. My gaze fell to his full lips before facing away again.

He approached my back and when I kneeled into position again, he reached between my legs ready to receive the ball. The top of his hand brushed against my sac in an obviously deliberate move.

"Torin," I warned, seconds away from embarrassing us both by tackling him to the ground and attacking his mouth.

"Accident." The lack of remorse in his voice should have tipped me off but the second time he did it, I growled low in my throat.

"I know what you are doing." Despite my warnings, I said nothing else as he continued to tease and tempt me with each snap, barely brushing my sensitive skin through my practice shorts. His touch felt too good, and I knew we were playing a dangerous game. I'd also developed a potentially embarrassing problem.

I jumped up. "I think we've practiced enough."

"Coach hasn't called it." He sounded genuinely upset but when I glanced at him he was smirking.

"Well when he does, I'd like to not approach him and the team with a raging hard-on."

He appeared proud of himself and I bumped his shoulder with mine.

After five minutes of back and forth, we must have regained Coach's attention. "You two enjoying your little break?"

"Back's cramping," I said in our defense. Averaging seventy snaps per game, I was used to the number of times we'd been at it. But the frequency was getting uncomfortable so I wasn't lying.

Coach nodded and for once did the *sane* thing. "That's enough then. I don't want to risk injury."

"Too bad," Torin murmured and I groaned.

TEN

TORIN

RUSH WAS SQUEEZING the steering wheel so hard his knuckles were turning white. His shoulders tensed and jaw clenched. I didn't utter a word the entire trip. I stared out the window as the sun set, sneaking discreet glances at the man next to me who appeared a bit unhinged.

After slamming his truck into park, he unclasped his seatbelt and I did mine. I stared after him as he jumped out of the truck, rounding the hood and strode to my side. He yanked the door open and gripped my hand. "Out."

He pressed his hand against my back and moved with urgency as he steered me toward our building. His truck beeped behind us and then he stuck his keys in his pocket, never slowing our pace.

"Um, Rush?" I questioned but let him keep his hand on my back as we took the steps two at a time. Once we got inside, I'd talk to him. Maybe I'd asked for too much too quick.

I fit my key into the lock and strong arms circled me around my waist. Warm lips met my neck and I shuddered as I slumped against him. Okay, not talking was fine. I reached back over his head, running my hands over his buzzed hair and holding him as his tongue darted out to taste me. I moaned loudly and Rush chuckled, his breath tickling my skin.

"Maybe we should go inside," he suggested and reached in front of me, turning the key and pushing the door open.

He guided me forward, softly shutting the door behind him. The sun had finished its descent and the room was bathed in shadows. The quiet highlighted every move and breath. Rush's solid chest pressed against my back as he ran his fingers up and down my arms. When I shivered he slowly spun me around and backed me up against the wall before slipping his arms around me again.

His hazel eyes stared into mine, fierce in the darkness. The way he looked at me reminded me of the first night I'd ever kissed him. I gulped at the intensity in his gaze.

Without warning, Rush's lips crashed against mine. The kiss wasn't soft. Years of pent-up desire and need spun out of control as he parted my lips with his tongue. I opened to him and he dove in. The kiss grew urgent as my hands wandered over his chest and gripped his shirt tight. My tongue massaged his as I tasted him like a man starved. His groans were loud and desperate, fueling my need for him. Despite the carnal way he took my mouth, it was infused with love. His arms banded tightly around me and he held me as if he'd never let go.

Rush suddenly pulled back just enough to look me in the eye. His gaze scanned over my face and he swallowed hard.

"You know I want you," he rasped. "Fuck, I always have, but I'm terrified of losing you."

"Never," I promised without a doubt in my mind.

His arms tightened around me and his palms slid to my

ass. "We won't be able to take it back. We'd be crossing a line we could never come back from."

"Good," I answered without an ounce of hesitancy.

His gaze heated. "You're mine."

"Always have been," I agreed.

He growled and dove back in, devouring my mouth. His hips ground against mine, letting me feel how hard he was as he pressed me against the wall. We both thrust hard and fast, seeking friction to ease our swollen cocks.

"You taste so fucking sweet," he groaned against my lips. "I want you naked so I can see, touch, and taste every inch of your bare skin."

"Yes," I hissed as he thrust hard.

Rush backed up and grabbed my hands, tugging me toward his bedroom. He flipped the switch on a small desk lamp so the room glowed in warm light.

I reached over my head and made sure I had his full attention before grabbing the back of my shirt and pulling it over my head. Rush copied the motion and I licked my lips. I stepped forward and ran my hands over his chest, down his abs and then made my way back up to thumb his dark nipples, feeling him shake beneath my touch. When I leaned forward and attached my lips around one, grazing it lightly with my teeth, he cursed.

Grabbing me by the shoulders, he straightened me and walked me back toward the bed. "Slow later. I need you now."

My cock jerked in response as I let him push me down onto the mattress. He wasted no time ripping down his shorts and boxers and kicking off his socks and shoes. His cock was huge and hard, like I already knew it was. Hell, I'd seen it enough times, but now I had permission to touch him. Because I worried he'd stop me if I didn't act fast, I leaned forward and took him into my mouth for the first time.

"Fucking hell." He groaned low and deep, immediately thrusting his hips, his length sliding between my tightly sealed lips. "You have the sweetest fucking mouth."

I had no idea what I was doing. My mouth was stretched wide and my jaw ached from trying to accommodate his thick girth. But every time he moaned, I redoubled my efforts, twisting my tongue, sucking harder.

His cock jerked and he pulled himself free. My first blow job and I'd nearly had Rush coming in mere minutes. If those weren't bragging rights... My thoughts froze when he prowled toward me.

I bit my lip as I watched him beneath hooded eyes as he pressed on my chest, urging me to lie back in the center of the bed. He climbed over me, crowding my space as he straddled my legs and propped himself up with one hand on the mattress.

Rush had caged me in. His lips were inches from mine, but he didn't offer them. Staring into my eyes, he slipped his fingers between us and unfastened my button. The *whir* of my zipper being lowered followed.

He backed down the bed until I had to prop myself up on my elbows to see what he was doing. After spreading my legs, he lay on his stomach between them and took hold of the band of my jeans. "Lift your hips," he whispered.

Shaking, I followed his instruction and arched my hips as he tugged the rough material and my boxers down just enough to reveal my hard shaft. Free of the material, it rested against my stomach, aching with a beaded drop of come forming at the tip.

Rush groaned and palmed my cock. "I've waited for this."

My eyes nearly rolled back. "Please don't tease me. I need you."

With a dark chuckle he closed his fingers around my hard flesh and stroked. My eyes slammed shut and a shudder ran through my body. Sucking on my bottom lip, I resisted the urge to thrust through the tight fist working me up and down. With my eyes closed, the warm, wet swipe of his tongue over my tip caught me off guard and dragged a moan from deep in my throat. The enveloping heat of Rush's mouth followed as he took me to the back of his throat until his lips wrapped tight around the base of my shaft. Once my cock was lodged deep, he swallowed.

"Rush," I begged, desperate to move my hips.

Then he sucked, dragging his mouth up my length in a slow, deliberate move. Unintelligible mumblings slipped between my lips as I thrust. I couldn't control my hips anymore. With his buzzed hair, I settled on the back of his head, loosely running my palms over the soft short hair as he bobbed up and down my length.

I opened my eyes to watch as he worshipped my cock, and the sight was something I'd never forget. As he swallowed me over and over he stared up into my eyes intently as if he'd been waiting for me to look at him. He sucked hard, and I panted as my balls drew tight. "If you don't stop, I'm going to come."

He pulled his mouth away and climbed off the bed. My questioning gaze followed him as he grabbed the bottom of my pants and yanked until he tugged them off fully, knocking my shoes off in the process with my socks following. He stripped me bare and then climbed over me.

He reached for the nightstand only a few feet away and pulled open the top drawer. When he pulled out a condom and lube, I swallowed hard. My legs shook and my heart raced. *Okay, this is happening.*

He set them on the bed and spread my legs, settling on his knees between them. He grabbed the condom between two fingers and held it up. "Are you sure, T? We can't—"

I huffed. "We can't take it back. I know, I know. Now get inside me."

"With fucking pleasure." He ripped open the condom wrapper and suited up before coating his fingers with the lube. Leaning over me, he used one arm to hold his weight as he kissed me. Slow and then fast, his kiss seemed to want to do it all and make up for all the years we'd spent denying ourselves.

The first touch of his slick finger against my hole made me cry out and my hips jerked up. Only his solid weight held me in place, rubbing our bodies together.

"I got you," he said and while he kissed me slow and deep, he circled my entrance until I relaxed.

"It feels so good." I moaned. "I can't believe it's you. Fucking, finally."

His words ghosted over my lips. "I know exactly what you mean."

Rush was patient as he waited for me to soften under his ministrations. When he felt I was ready, his breached my entrance with a slow, persistent push. My walls stretched as he smoothly slid his finger into me, creating a slight burn.

"Oh, fuck," I panted. The mixture of pleasure with a small bite of pain was too much, and my hips rolled. Rush fingered me, showing me how good it could feel with only a small part of him. I could only imagine how it would feel to have him replace his finger with something much larger. I reached for my cock that had leaked onto my stomach.

"Not yet." His voice was strained. "Wait until I'm inside you. Watching your face as you ride my finger is killing me. Let me in."

With that he added a second finger, the burning pressure quickly giving way to pleasure. By the time he added the third finger I was so gone, I barely felt the burn, just the deep pleasure his fingers were giving me as he rubbed me inside. Knowing how fucking big his dick was, I appreciated him taking the time to prep me well, but I was done waiting.

I squirmed beneath him and gazed up into his hazel eyes. "Rush, I'm ready."

He shook above me and his breathing was harsh as he removed his fingers and leaned back on his knees. I watched in rapt attention as he uncapped the lube again and applied a generous amount to his cock. He wrapped his hand around his width, jacking his cock as he coated himself. My mouth dropped open. I'd never wanted anything as badly as I wanted him to fill me. To connect to him on that deep of a level.

When he lay back on top of me I pulled my knees back slightly, giving him better access.

"Torin?" He was trembling on top of me.

"Yeah?" I whispered and my teeth chattered.

"You know I love you, right?"

My heart burst in my chest. "I know, though I admit I still enjoy hearing it. I feel the same way." Wrapping my hand around his neck, I drew him down. Just before his lips met mine, I whispered, "I love you back."

He paused and gripped my chin, holding my gaze. "No, T, I'm in love with you."

"Jesus, Rush, are you trying to make me cry?" I yanked him down and kissed him hard until we were both breathless. "I'm in love with you too. Now please get inside of me."

He reached between us and lined his tip with my entrance. Holding my gaze, he pressed in, applying pressure as he breached the ring of muscle. I gasped at the intrusion and he froze.

"Good?" he said with a strained tone as he held himself back.

I made myself relax. "I am now. Give me more."

He slipped deeper into me, my channel clenching around him. His grunts of approval encouraged me to tilt my hips to better our angle, allowing him slide in to the hilt.

"Fuuuuck," he gritted through his teeth and rested his forehead against mine. "You feel amazing. Better than I ever imagined."

"You imagined?" I traced my fingers over his back, loving the feel of Rush inside me, something I'd never share with anyone else.

He pulled his hips back and I clenched around him. Dipping down to taste my neck, he then whispered in my ear. "You didn't?"

"All the time." He thrust and I cried out. "All the damn time."

His hips moved in a steady rhythm as I got used to the feeling. One place deep inside me was driving me crazy each time his cock slid over it. "That feels so good. Faster."

"I shouldn't. Not yet." He seemed to be trying to convince himself.

"Damn it, Rush—"

My words were cut off when his slow deep thrusts quickened until he fucked me fast and hard. "I swear I'll take you slow next time. You have no idea how bad I needed this. How long I've wanted it."

"I think I have an idea." My heels dug into his ass as I

urged him on. My cock was full on leaking onto my stomach as he rubbed that spot with each snap of his hips.

I reached between us and didn't even get to touch my aching cock before his hand knocked mine away. "Don't. I want it all."

He jacked me with perfectly timed stokes. Each slide of his thick girth mimicked the way he handled my cock.

"I'm not going to last," I warned.

"Don't then." He worked me faster and fucked me harder. "Come for me."

I'd been waiting for this for years so when my orgasm hit, it was like a blinding flash of lightning, the roar of the ocean in my ears, my body felt as if it'd been lit on fire and my cock pulsed as I was consumed by the earth-shattering feeling of finally giving everything to my best friend. The last piece was now completely his.

"You are sexy as fuck when you come." He groaned loud and his hips jerked. His eyes closed and mouth dropped open in a silent moan as he slammed inside me once more before stilling. Aftershocks wracked his body making him jerk on top of me. Slowly, he opened his eyes right before his arms gave way, and he barely caught himself before we crashed into each other. "Shit, am I dead?"

I chuckled as Rush slipped out of me and rolled onto the mattress. His movements were lazy as he turned his head toward me with a goofy grin.

After recovering, he took care of the condom and left the room, returning with a wash cloth he used to clean the mess we'd made. He tossed it in the laundry hamper before jumping back in bed, scooping me into his arms.

Rush's large build had always made me feel secure, but in his embrace I felt untouchable. Minutes later, soft snores filled the room and a small smile spread over my face as I watched Rush's face relaxed in sleep. Still in a state of disbelief, if it weren't for the delicious ache in my ass, I might not believe it ever happened.

Pressing closer to him, I wiggled one of my legs between his. In his sleep, he still lifted just enough to give me room to tangle us together. With the comfort of him surrounding me, I fell into the best sleep of my life.

ELEVEN
RUSH

THE TWO HUNDRED pound quarterback lying on top of me was making me overheat in the unfamiliar hotel bed. The sheets were twisted around our bodies from rolling around in them until the early morning hours, which didn't help. Torin was fast asleep, so I took a minute to study his face. His full lips parted a sliver, his hair in disarray and his eyelashes sweeping down over his tanned skin. Torin was fucking beautiful. And he was mine.

After a four and a half hour bus ride to northern Oklahoma on Thanksgiving Day, we'd stopped by the hotel and dropped off our stuff. Then we'd gone out in search of somewhere open so we could grab something to eat, but everything was already closed. The hotel took pity on us and served us some decent holiday food.

Thinking of food made my stomach growl, and I could imagine the smell of turkey and dressing back home.

We had to be on the bus at noon and needed to get up. As I turned enough to snag my phone from the dark cherry wood night stand, he stirred against me. When I read the time, I cursed. We'd slept in and I'd miss my alarm.

"Wake up, T. We're running late." I shook his shoulder.

"What?" He lids cracked open and he focused on my face.

"We slept in."

His eyes widened and he jumped out of bed and ran to the bathroom. I heard the sink turn on and frowned. *Where's my morning kiss?*

I forced myself out of bed, went into the bathroom where Torin was standing at the sink, brushing his teeth, and I jumped in to take a quick shower. Then we switched places. He turned the heat up on the water and scrubbed the smell of sex down the drain, as I brushed my teeth and dragged a razor across the stubble on my face.

Torin was always faster than me, and he sprinted into the bedroom. "Hurry up," he said as I finished up in the bathroom.

He was already tying his shoelaces when I came out, so I threw on some shorts and a Saints' t-shirt before lacing mine. Our gear was already packed, and the rest would already be on the bus, so I grabbed our game bags.

"Ready?" He stood by the door, holding it open.

"Yup, let's go." I shouldered my bag and handed Torin his as I walked by. "Forgetting something?"

He snatched the bag. "Thank you."

I chuckled as I pulled the door shut and stuck our keycard in my pocket. We hurried to the elevator and jogged toward the lobby, making a pit stop by the breakfast buffet. I grabbed a couple of sausage and egg sandwiches and two large cartons of orange juice, passing one of each to Torin. We raced out into the parking lot just as the last of our team was loading onto the bus.

"Glad you two decided to join us." Coach Sanders stood with his arms crossed.

"Sorry." I climbed the stairs and strode straight for the back of the bus. When I sat down, Torin took the spot next to me. I needed to get my head in the game, so I grabbed my MP3 player out of my bag and hooked up my earbuds. I shoved one in my ear and the other I handed to Torin who put it in his. I handed him the device so he could choose the song and started bobbing my head when he made a solid choice.

Not even ten minutes later, we were pulling into the Tigers' iconic stadium.

As we filed off the bus, I let Torin lead and I trailed behind as we made our way to the visiting locker room.

Each player went through their pregame routines and rituals. I turned my music back on, but unplugged the earbuds and turned up the volume. Several hoots echoed in the room as the fast bass thumped through the cavernous room.

I slipped on my pads as Torin did the same.

"How are you feeling?" He asked as he slid on his pants.

I pulled on my undershirt. "Good, I think. If you're wondering if I'm still hung up on the last game, I'm not. Just ready to get out there. What about you? Feeling good?"

"Well, my ass is still sore. Want to kiss it better?"

My gaze jerked back to his blue eyes, wide and feigning innocence. Torin bit his lip and winked.

"Jesus, T. I'm not in the best situation for a boner." I indicated my bulge and he grinned. I hid my own smile. "Besides you hurt my feelings this morning. I thought for sure I'd get a wake up kiss, so I think you should kiss me instead."

He appeared pleased with himself for riling me up. Then he glanced around the room. My gaze automatically followed and noted our teammates caught up in their own thing. Torin darted in, pressing an unexpected hard but quick kiss on my lips.

Shocked, I gaped at him. "I didn't mean right now." Not that I gave a shit if anyone saw, but it'd take some getting used to. Though it wasn't a secret I was bisexual, they probably didn't suspect anything between me and Torin.

"First you complain that I didn't kiss you and now you complain when I do. I'm starting to think boyfriends are overrated. High-maintenance ass." He rolled his eyes and sighed.

Meanwhile, my world stopped spinning.

"Boyfriend?" I tried out the word, feeling it on my lips and tasting it on my tongue.

"Well, yeah," he said as if it was the most obvious thing in the world. "I mean we are, right? All things considered."

"Boyfriend," I repeated this time with a nod, letting the word and meaning sink in.

"You should see your face," Torin said, as he resumed getting ready, pulling the rest of his pads on. "You okay over there?" He snickered.

The sound was infectious and I found myself chuckling with him, sending him a wink. Lightness filled me, and I felt like a piece I'd been missing clicked into place.

"Let's play some ball!" I hollered and the team joined in. Torin slipped his Saints jersey on and waited for me to finish before we made our way to the circle of players surrounding Coach Sanders.

"Pipe down and listen," he began, and we gave him our undivided attention. "The Sugar Land Saints have had a great deal of success, but I believe this is the best team the program has seen in a long time. Maybe ever." Everyone cheered and he held up a staying hand until we quieted. "Win this game and leave as victors! Then enjoy a nice weekend, before training like your lives depend on it for the next game, the game that decides whether we make the playoffs." His eyes met each of ours briefly. "This is a big game with high stakes and bigger reward. Some of you remember, or even played, the game against the Tigers last year. We lost and it kept us out of the playoffs. We may have lost last year, but today we change that. Today we win! Then we keep winning until we make it to the championship game."

"Fuck yeah," Nash yelled across the circle from us and the room exploded in noise.

Coach smiled. "Well, get your asses up. It's time to make these fuckers say uncle." His lips twitched. "But I never said that."

"No, sir," we all shouted and laughed.

A cacophony of sounds coming from the stadium—spectators, vendors, media, bands and cheerleaders—traveled all the way down the tunnel and into the locker room. It was crazy. The Saints always had a good showing of support from family and fans, but so did the Tigers. Between the two, the stadium had completely sold out. Things would be deafening and intense right from the get-go.

Excitement sent chills running up and down my spine. This was the feeling I lived for. The spike of adrenaline, feeding off the crowd's energy, was like nothing else. I glanced over to Torin. Well, almost like nothing else. He met my eyes as if he felt my stare, and his gaze heated. I couldn't wait to get him back to the hotel, preferably on the high of a big win.

I winked. "Are you ready?"

"You know it." He smirked, but then it dimmed.

"What's wrong?" It was difficult not to reach out and

touch him. We hadn't talked about how we wanted to handle outing our relationship.

"You're going to get drafted. You are too good not to."

I waited for the rest because I didn't understand why that seemed to bother him.

"You realize I will be coming with you, right?" His steady gaze spoke of love and resolve.

"You want to talk about that now?" My eyebrows shot high.

"There's nothing to talk about. It's happening." His tone was firm. "I was just making sure you knew."

My grin stretched wide and I chuckled because damn, I felt like I'd already won. "Understood." I saluted him.

"Good," he said, and finally shared my smile.

A representative for the Tigers showed up to tell us it was time to go and we filed down the tunnel behind Coach. We broke into a run once we hit open crisp air and the bright sun that did nothing to cut the bite of the wind. Perfect football weather.

The crowd screamed, yelled and booed as the sea of black and gold Saints invaded the field. The sounds were intoxicating.

"Let's do this!" Shaw yelled as he and Bishop jogged next to us toward our side of the field.

MY UNDERSHIRT STUCK to my body as sweat coated my skin.

The two-minute warning was called and the clock stopped ticking down. With only one hundred and twenty seconds left of the game, I felt the pressure. I'd fucked up royally at the same moment during the last game and I promised myself to keep my guard up. Getting through me to get to Torin would take a fucking miracle, and I hoped the guy across from me wasn't expecting divine intervention because it wasn't happening. Despite being up by fourteen, it wasn't unheard of for the other team to have an extraordinary comeback.

My fingers gripped the ball as I held it in place against the turf. One more first down and we could run down the clock, ending the game and taking home the win. One more play, I reminded myself.

"Set," Torin yelled and then grunted behind me. I snapped the ball.

The Saints created a wall and surged forward as a black and gold wave pushed the Tigers back. Torin tucked the ball tight to his body and used us as a shield as he bulldozed his way into me, helping drive me forward. *We just need one fucking yard.*

With the muscle behind the Tigers, the play ended in a tangle of limbs as refs from every angle raced to the pile. They began pulling players up to find the football. Weight was lifted from my body as Torin got up. I peeked at the ref just as he signaled we'd done it.

Torin reached for my hand and, with a giant grin, helped pull me up as the chains were moved and we were granted a fresh set of downs. All we needed to do was run the clock down. The seconds ticked by through four plays as a formality, and the game was called. The Saints were headed to the playoffs. *Hell, yes!*

We ran off the field into our other teammates, colliding mid-air into each other and slapping palms.

"Shit!" I heard Coach yell and glanced over to see him soaking wet as Shaw and Nash each held a side to a giant orange cooler. The whole team grinned and cracked up.

The Tigers met us mid-field in a disordered group for pats on the back and congratulations. Though they'd been beaten, most were good sports and my respect for the team grew. But today was ours and I was ready to celebrate with Torin.

Reporters surrounded many of the players who made key plays, one of course being Torin as he did his obligatory quarterback interview. His beautiful face was animated as he talked about the game, and my attention never left him. I watched as the women around him melted on the spot. It was the smile, I decided.

Though I was pumped, it was hard to ignore the exhaustion, and I was ready to get out of the sweaty uniform. I waited on Torin, and after cleaning up and changing, we dragged our asses back to the hotel for which I was extremely grateful. Due to freezing conditions throughout a large part of Oklahoma, Sugar Land had allowed us to remain for one more night before taking the bus back to Texas in the morning.

TWELVE

TORIN

RUSH and I tumbled onto the bed in our hotel room, the crisp sheets beneath us were cool and the room smelled of fresh linen.

What started as a sweet kiss morphed into a heated frenzy of hands tearing at clothes. My exhaustion and aches vanished as I sat up and yanked my shirt off. Rush dug his fingers into my blond hair that was still damp from the shower and dragged me back down so he could thoroughly fuck my mouth with his tongue.

Abruptly he ended the kiss. "Stand up."

My pulse increased as excitement ran through my veins. I climbed off of him and followed his instruction. "Now what?"

He lifted onto his elbows and studied me while biting his bottom lip. When I tried to unbutton my jeans, he sat up and grabbed my hand. "Let me."

He slipped the button free and then the *whir* of the zipper being pulled down gave me chills. His movements were slow and deliberate, taking in every moment. He took his time peeling my jeans off and then running his hands up my bare legs.

After he'd stripped off my boxers, he crooked his finger, beckoning me to come even closer. Something about being exposed while he remained dressed excited me. He'd put me on display just for him. I shivered as I crawled into his lap, straddling him. Rush was so big that even at my size, I didn't feel like I was crushing him.

Face to face, I leaned forward and bit his bottom lip. He groaned as he reached between us and circled my nipple with his finger until it hardened into a stiff peak before doing the same to the other.

"You are so fucking sexy. It was a miracle I kept my hands off you for as long as I did." His already rough voice sounded like it had clawed its way over sharp jagged rocks.

"Well I'd appreciate it if you put them on me a little more." I grabbed his hands and pulled them around me, lowering them to my ass and encouraging him to grip me. He obliged. His large hands cupped my ass as he pulled me closer until we rubbed together, cock to cock, chest to chest. I squirmed. "Take your clothes off."

He let go of me and I leaned back on his thighs to watch him lift his shirt over his head. I'd never get tired of ogling his body, big and broad, his nipples dark and flat, and the way he looked at me melted my heart.

"Up," he commanded and maneuvered me off his lap. He lay on the bed and undid his pants, lifted his hips and tugged them down, taking his boxers with them.

"Oh, fuck," I moaned. His thick cock lay hard against his belly, come leaking from the darkened tip.

"Get the lube and a condom from my wallet." His voice shook.

I reached down and into the pocket of his jeans, grabbing what I needed. I straddled his lap again and began to rip open the condom. He grabbed it from me.

"I wanted to do that," I complained, but my words caught in my throat when he rolled the rubber down my length. Knowing he'd never bottomed, I gaped at him. "What are you doing?"

He gave me a look that said *"really?"* but I honestly needed clarification. I'd never imagined fucking him and the idea made my cock jerk in response.

"You want me to fuck you?" I swallowed hard around the knot that had formed in my throat.

"No," he said gruffly, his face heated into a deep red as he stared into my eyes. "I want you to love me."

I went boneless on top of him, my heavy weight lying over his chest and stomach. The kiss I planted on his lips was slow and sensual. "I do love you," I murmured against his lips.

"Then show me," he whispered back.

He was prepared to give me something he'd never given anyone else and the trust that came with his admission was immense.

Because he appeared to be nervous about the request, I didn't make a thing of it. We'd talk later. Right now, the only thing I wanted to do was give him exactly what he asked for. And then I wanted him to return the favor. And then I wanted to do it for the rest of our lives. Fast, slow, rough or soft, I'd give him everything every single time.

I lifted off of his body, returning to standing.

"Spread." I coaxed him with a hand on the inside of his thigh. His legs shook as he slowly complied though his face was still flushed. As soon as I saw his pink hole, I groaned. "So fucking sexy."

He seemed to relax at my words and opened farther, tilting his hips and gaining confidence.

I tore open the small package of lube, generously coating first my cock and then my fingers.

"Rush..." I breathed out. My words trailed off as I reached forward and skimmed my fingers over his cock, his sac, down his taint and then touched him for the first time. He gasped and then groaned as I circled his hole. Adding light pressure, I grazed his puckered flesh. He was extremely sensitive, I discovered. He lifted his hips over and over, seeking more as I gave him free reign to move as he wanted. He drove me crazy and I wanted to bury my finger inside of him. I lay a firm hand on his belly and pressed down until his back was flat on the bed and his movements slowed. "Hold still and relax. Let me in."

I added more pressure this time, slipping the tip of my finger inside. He tensed and clenched around my finger. "Breathe."

"Okay," he panted and a moment later his hold on my finger loosened.

I drove forward in a slick smooth entry, burying my finger completely and then crooked it. His hips shot up and a string of curses flowed from his mouth. I massaged the sensitive place inside. I loved it when he'd done it to me but was surprised how much he seemed to like it too. He chanted my name over and over.

"Don't come," I gritted out and stopped rubbing. Instead, I slowly fingered him. He was so damn tight that when I attempted to add a second finger, it took a lot of coaxing to get him to relax and breathe before I managed to slide the digit in. He hissed at the intrusion but soon rode my fingers like he couldn't get enough. "One more, and then I'm going to slide inside you."

He groaned deep in his throat. "Yes."

Slowly we worked together to insert my third finger, stretching him and adding more lube. When I thought he was ready, I positioned myself between his legs and lined up my tip to his hole. "Ready?"

"Get inside me, T. Stop fucking around." His hands went to my ass as he attempted to pull me inside of him.

I grinned as I pushed slowly into him. "Holy fucking shit," I muttered and my eyes rolled back. "So damn tight."

At first, Rush's fingers dug into my arms as if he wasn't sure he wanted more, but when I retreated, he gripped me harder, tugging me closer. "Don't you dare," he warned.

When I thrust deeper, sliding against the spot that drove him crazy, he clenched and moaned. Things almost ended before they began as I held still, holding off my orgasm.

Once I'd gained control and he'd adjusted to my size, he encouraged me. Slowly rocking my hips, my cock slid in shallow then deep as I kissed him and murmured how good he felt and how much he meant to me. When he wanted it harder, I gave it to him. Each time I went deep he grunted and dug his blunt nails into my back.

"Fuck, I'm gonna come," I warned and reached between us, stroking his cock tight and fast.

His mouth dropped open in a silent 'oh' and his eyes slammed shut as his come shot all over my hand and our stomachs.

It was all I needed to send me over and I came hard, emptying myself inside my boyfriend. My best friend.

Once our breathing calmed, I slowly and carefully slipped from his body and cursed when he winced in pain.

"You okay?" My brow furrowed and I rubbed his arm soothingly.

"Sore, but totally worth it."

I leaned down and kissed him, slow and soft. He smiled against my lips and my heart swelled. I pulled away and grabbed tissues from the box on the nightstand and cleaned us up. "Be right back."

"Uh, huh," he muttered as his eyelids drooped. Rush curled on his side and hugged the pillow.

My skin was slick from sweat as I climbed from the bed and crossed the room. I tossed the condom in the trash and washed my hands before grabbing the empty ice bucket that sat in the nook next to a coffee pot. "I'm going to run and grab ice. Do you need anything?"

He sleepily waved me off and I grinned as I slid back into my clothes.

After grabbing my keycard and the bucket, I left the room, searching for signs that would point me in the right direction and found my way to the vending area. Just as I set my bucket to fill, I heard Shaw's voice.

"Come on," he coaxed in a low voice and then groaned. "Stay with me tonight. No one will know."

His room must have been just across the hall and I wasn't surprised he'd found someone for the night. There were always girls ready and willing after games, especially if you won. Like we were a prize to be claimed and, for some, bragged about.

I didn't want to throw off his game by turning on the loud ass ice machine, so I opted to stay quiet and hope they moved on. Bishop's lowered raspy voice surprised me because I hadn't expected it.

"Keep fucking jacking my cock and I'll do more than stay with you tonight. You want me to fuck you?"

Shaw hissed. "Yes."

"Are you going to do everything I tell you to?"

Shaw's moan was followed by the slamming of a door, so I could only assume he'd agreed, but holy shit. Shaw and Bishop! Why was I even surprised? Things clicked into place. The way Shaw listened when Bishop spoke, and the way the dark prince was always watching Shaw as if he couldn't look away if he wanted to.

I peeked around the corner and confirmed the hall was empty. I quickly filled the ice and sprinted back to our room in case one of them came back out and discovered me. I hadn't tried to pry into their business.

"Whoa, where's the fire?" Rush jerked upright when I ran in, closing the door harder than necessary.

I chuckled. "Apparently in Shaw's and Bishop's pants."

Rush tilted his head and studied me as if I'd lost my mind.

Grabbing a plastic cup from the nook I poured ice into it and made my way back to the bed. "Did you know they were fucking?"

"Really? I had no clue." He sat up fully when I offered him an ice chip and put one in my mouth. "How do you know?"

"Shaw's room was right across from the ice machine. I thought he was talking to a girl and didn't want to ruin his game or whatever. But it wasn't a girl, it was Bishop and it was very clear what they were about to do. Or in the middle of doing. Apparently Bishop's bossy in the sack."

"I can't decide whether it makes perfect sense or a tragedy in the making," Rush said and opened his mouth, silently asking for more ice. I tilted the cup and let a piece slide onto his tongue.

"Agreed." But my thoughts turned back to Rush and what had happened between us. It was one of the most amazing moments in my life.

After I set the cup down on the nightstand, I slipped back out of my clothes and into bed next to him. Propping my elbow on the mattress, I rested my head on my hand and peered up into his hazel eyes. "Why did you let me top you? You told me you never do that."

He lay down alongside me and ran a finger over my cheek. "With you, I want everything." He curled his body around mine and yawned. "And I trust you."

My throat tightened as I eased down to my pillow and pressed in closer to him.

As my eyes began to close and Rush's breathing deepened, my thoughts turned to the weekend and going home. What would our parents think? The thought made me chuckle.

"What?" he asked in a grumpy whisper.

"Just thinking about telling our families about us."

He pulled me tighter to him. "It will be okay. *We'll* be okay. My family loves you and I know I'm part of yours."

"But your dad—"

"We'll be fine, T. Now turn that sexy brain of yours off and go to sleep with me."

"My sexy... brain?" I snorted.

He gave me a drowsy half-grin. "Shut up and go to sleep."

Happier than I'd ever been, I curled in farther and inhaled deep, the scent of Rush's spicy cologne lulling me to sleep.

THIRTEEN
RUSH

THE TRIP HOME was rowdier than the ride to Oklahoma. Music blared from phones, and MP3 players, loud chatter and laughter competed with the bus's roaring engine. Torin and I leaned against each other in the back seat, content to observe the madness.

Torin ended up falling asleep halfway through the drive and slouched over, using my shoulder as a pillow. We got a few glances, but no one said anything. They all knew we were close, so it wasn't anything new.

When we were about ten minutes away from the campus, I shook Torin's shoulder. "Wake up."

He woke up slowly, casting me a lazy grin, and I returned it.

Shaw lifted himself to his knees on his bench a few rows up. "Who is coming tonight? Bishop's dad is inviting the whole team, and if you want to bring someone, he said that's fine. He's reserved the whole second floor."

"As long as they aren't assholes," Bishop added without looking up from typing on his phone.

Shaw rolled his eyes and added, "No assholes."

Most of the team decided they were going, but we reminded them that we'd be leaving as soon as we got back to campus. We were both ready to see our families.

"Why do I always find it slightly disturbing when Bishop speaks?" I whispered.

Torin chuckled. "You'd think after three years we'd be used to it, huh?"

I chuckled under my breath. "Rich odd fucker."

We both considered Bishop a friend though it was hard to know someone so reserved. Still, he was good people as far as I was concerned

"I could use a nap." I yawned and stretched my arms.

"Me too," Torin agreed echoing my yawn.

"You've been sleeping."

"I'm still tired." He leaned up and kissed me.

I gripped his chin to hold him still as I nipped his bottom lip. "So, you're saying I have to drive to Riverside?"

Nash's voice cut through our conversation. "So are you guys like publicly out now as a couple?"

And then I realized we'd kissed in public for the first time, and it definitely had been more than friendly. I glanced around, noticing we'd gained a lot of attention before focusing back on Nash. "What do you mean *now*?"

He slow blinked and spoke slowly. "Like the down low shit y'all have been doing for like, I don't know, ever."

My eyebrows shot high and I glanced at Torin. "We got together like five minutes ago."

Nash appeared skeptical and Torin cleared his throat.

"We did," I insisted, looking at Nash. Then I glanced down at Torin's fake pout. "Not five minutes literally, stop being dramatic."

"Huh," Nash said while unwrapping a sucker.

"Look," I said, darting a look to each of my teammates. "We don't owe anyone an explanation."

"Stop getting defensive. I'm glad you guys are together. You were driving us all a little crazy, wondering what you two's deal was." And then he stuck the sucker in his mouth.

I glanced at Shaw who was leaning over the back of his seat, nodding in agreement. Bishop's black gaze just flicked from me to Torin.

The bus pulled into the campus parking lot and we unloaded. We took Torin's Jeep back to the apartment and packed new bags for the weekend before jumping in my truck to make another long drive.

"I GOT IT," I called out as I climbed off the worn brown leather couch where my dad and I were lounging, watching a football game. My stomach growled as I passed the kitchen and peeked in. Mom was doing something to the turkey in the oven and it smelled amazing. After I'd dropped Torin off at his parents' house, I'd come straight home and been tortured with smelling food I wasn't allowed to eat yet.

I crossed the room and swung the door open, only to feel like I'd been slapped in the face. John, my uncle, stood on the other side with a small smile.

"Happy Thanksgiving, Rush," he said and shuffled in place. "I'm sorry to show up unannounced, but I hoped you would be here for the holiday weekend."

"What are you doing here? Were you invited?" I was in shock and not thrilled that he was intruding on our family's tradition.

"Ah, not exactly..."

"Who's at the door, honey?" My mom stepped behind me and placed her hand on my arm. "John," she clipped out.

"Hi, Angela, I don't mean to ruin your holiday weekend. It's just that things have changed for me lately and I hoped I could talk to Rush for a few minutes." His gaze returned to me.

My dad walked up about the same time. He nodded at his brother.

"Joel." My uncle tilted his head. "I'm sorry for just showing up. I was afraid you might say no if I called. I'd like to talk to Rush for just a few minutes if he'd be okay with that."

"How about you talk to me first?" my dad challenged, but I cut in. If he just needed a few minutes, we should get this over with and he could be on his way.

I stepped outside onto the wood deck. "It's fine."

Other than a questioning look on their faces, they said nothing, but I knew it would be eating them alive, wondering why John was there. I was curious too.

"Sit with me on the steps?" he asked and I agreed by taking a seat on the top one.

We sat in silence for a moment. A cool breeze shook leaves free from the trees and I watched as they drifted down onto the piles that needed bagging.

"Not to be overly rude, but what are you doing here, John, if you weren't invited?" I broke the silence.

He breathed heavily. "I owe you an apology. Hell, I owe a lot of apologies, but I want to start with you. The way I abandoned you and your mom is unforgiveable. I'm not making excuses, but I wanted to tell you how very sorry I am," he repeated.

I settled my elbows on my knees and steepled my hands. My gaze strayed to Lucy who stood by the fence as if watching us, but actually probably wanted an apple. "Say what you need to say then."

"You got that bluntness from your mama," he mused, but when I didn't respond, he cleared his throat.

"I'm not sure what your mama told you, and hopefully I'm not screwing this up by telling you, but when she got pregnant, I was hooked on some bad shit. Excuse my language." He briefly glanced at me, and I noted for the first time how clear his eyes looked. John also smelled of cologne. When he stayed with us before, he smelled like booze was oozing out of his pores.

I shrugged. "You're worried about leaving a bad impression?" I lifted a brow and he gave a humorless chuckle.

"I'm sober. I've been sober for two years now, but I didn't want to approach you until I knew I could stay on track. Between my sponsor and surrounding myself with a different crowd, I finally believe I can do it. I feel better than I have in my whole life. Looking back, I can't believe the things it cost me. Your mother. You." He sniffed and a quick dab at his nose with his shirt sleeve and got control of himself. "Rush, I am so, so sorry. I know it doesn't make it right and I can't change things."

That wasn't what I'd expected his visit to be about. After a moment, I recognized that he expected a response.

"I understand," I said, because I had no idea what to say. "I've had a good life," I said, trying to make him feel better. I wasn't even mad. Four years after finding out, I'd thought about it a lot, and regardless of John's abandonment, I'd had a good life. Sure, it sucked that I'd been lied to, but the alternative was a drug-addicted parent and for that, I was grateful to my dad. For stepping up. For loving me even though I wasn't biologically his.

The door creaked behind us, and I glanced over my

shoulder to where my dad peeked out. "Everything all right, Rush?"

"I'm good, Dad."

He eyed me as if trying to see if I was telling the truth, and must have decided I was okay, because he went back inside.

"Does it bother you to hear me call him *dad*?" I asked, trying to see it from his point of view, not that it truly mattered.

He was silent for a moment. "I feel a lot of things when I hear it. There's anger at myself, relief for you, gratitude for my brother. It's confusing, but I have done it to myself. Your dad loves you and gave you a much better life than I ever could have."

More silence passed as I considered and finally accepted his words. "Okay."

"Okay?" he asked.

"Sure, I mean if you're here to apologize, then I accept."

He breathed long and loud, and his voice shook when he spoke. "Do you think you could still call me Uncle John? I know that's a lot to ask. But I hoped now that I'm sober I might, I don't know, keep in contact sometimes. When you're up to it. Your pace and whatever you're comfortable with."

My heart picked up pace, matching the almost panicked verbal spewing coming from my uncle. I felt my face flush and sweat rolled down my neck. "Maybe we'll play it one day at a time," I suggested. This conversation was too new, too heavy, for me to commit to anything. I wasn't sure I wanted any type of relationship with him. I needed to talk to someone. Someone who understood me better than I understood myself sometimes. I needed Torin.

"I have somewhere to be," I said as I stood.

"I reckon I better tell your mom and dad why I'm here, before she has a conniption fit. She's been watching us this whole time."

I chuckled briefly as we stood, and I opened the door, holding it open for him.

My mom and dad stood side-by-side.

"Can we talk?" my uncle asked.

"I think that would be best," my mom said with a troubled expression. I grabbed my keys. "Where are you headed?"

"Torin's. But I'll be back before supper."

"You can't be separated for more than a few hours," she said knowingly.

But I just needed to have him listen. He grounded me. Everything made more sense when I shared my problems with him.

"Torin?" my uncle asked. "Wasn't that the boy you played football with in high school? He was there that day?"

"We still play football together and he's my boyfriend," I said with a straight face, shocking myself with my outburst.

John nodded slowly. "Well, one day I hope to meet him under better conditions."

"We'll see." I gave him a tight smile and then glanced to my parents. "I'll be back in a few."

"Okay, love you, honey." My mom and dad both wore confused expressions. I hadn't told them about Torin and me yet. We'd planned on doing it together the next day. I hoped he wasn't upset. I definitely hadn't meant to do it.

"You too." I got in my truck, and took off down the long driveway a little faster than usual, small chunks of broken rocks were thrown from my spinning tires.

"WHAT'S WRONG?" Torin asked when he opened the door and read the uncertainty on my face. He grabbed me by the arm and tugged me inside. As he led me upstairs, I caught a brief glimpse of his mom.

"Rush, dear, are you staying to eat?" Her words halted my progress and I stepped back down a few stairs. Her blond hair was up in a bun and her pixie like features lit up with a smile.

"No, ma'am. I'm just here to talk to Torin for a minute before I have to head home. I'll be here tomorrow like usual though."

The plan had been to spend Saturday with our separate families and then Sunday to tell them each about our relationship, but I'd decimated those plans about ten minutes before when I spilled the beans before walking out.

"You'd better." She put her hands on her hips and winked. "We've been slaving over this peach cobbler."

"Yes ma'am. I'd never miss my favorite," I promised.

"All right, you boys run off and do whatever you need to. I'm done intruding." She turned back and disappeared into the kitchen.

"You're never intruding," I called back as Torin rolled his eyes and then pulled me upstairs.

"Don't give her permission or we'll be down there for hours."

He led me to his room and then locked us inside. I sat on his bed. It felt weird because the soft navy blue comforter was straightened neatly and not rumpled from use like it always was when he lived there. He leaned against the wall. "Tell me what's wrong."

"Well two things." I rubbed the back of my head. "I sort of let slip that you were my boyfriend."

His expression turned thoughtful. "Well, I guess that saves that awkward talk."

"Um, not exactly." I grimaced. "I left right after I said it."

He burst out laughing. "Well, I guess it will be interesting then."

"My uncle showed up." I smoothed my hand over the blanket.

He sobered immediately and pushed off the wall to sit next to me. He grabbed my hand. "After four years of silence, why would he do that?"

I sighed. "He wanted to talk. I think to get some things off his chest and maybe alleviate some guilt or something. He's sober or at least he says he is. He looks sober."

Torin threaded his fingers through mine. "Is he staying?"

"I don't think so. He stayed behind to talk to my parents after I left."

"That why you stormed out?"

"I didn't exactly storm out. I said I was coming here. He asked if you were the boy I played football with, and with all of them standing there, I blurted out that you were my boyfriend." I winced and rubbed my temple. "You're not mad are you?"

"Not even a little." He leaned forward and pressed a kiss to my neck.

"I fucking love you." Wrapping my arm around him, I pulled him against me.

He rested his head on my chest and our hands in my lap. "I know. Just like you know I love you."

"I needed... you. I'm sorry to like intrude on your family time."

He scoffed. "I'm pretty sure they already think of you as a son. Want to go tell them now? Even the score?"

It would be easiest to just put it out there. Our relationship wasn't going anywhere. "I think I do."

He stood and tugged on my hand. "They won't have a problem with it. We both know that. But even if they did, it wouldn't matter. You know that, right?"

I grabbed the back of his neck, dragging him to me and pressed our lips together in a short, heated kiss. "I know. And I can't wait to get you alone."

He groaned. "Don't tease me."

I let him lead me from his room and back downstairs where his dad sat in a chair watching some old western movie, and his mom busied herself in the kitchen, preparing for tomorrow's feast. "Mom, can you come here for a second? There's something I, *we* need to tell you."

She appeared from the kitchen drying her hands on a dishtowel. "Sure, is everything all right?"

Her gaze bounced between the two of us as she sat on the arm of the army green chair Torin's dad lounged in. His arm immediately circled her waist as he also turned his attention to us. Quite a bit older than her, he had a full head of white hair, was as tall as Torin and had a calm demeanor.

We didn't need to say much. Torin still had a firm grip on my hand. I squeezed back and he glanced over and winked.

"You two?" she asked with a neutral expression.

His dad scowled. "All those times you stayed the night were you two—"

"Dad! No, and it's a little late getting on to me, even if that had happened. It's new. Well, new and old, I guess."

He shrugged, appearing lost for words. He glanced to me for help.

"Right, new and old," I agreed with a nod.

Torin snorted, and his parents smiled.

"Well, I can say I'm only a little surprised," he said as he seemed to consider the situation. "You could have come to us and told us you were gay, Torin. We would have supported you."

Torin pinched the bridge of his nose. "Well, there wasn't anything to tell at the time. I'm not gay."

His parents both appeared confused.

"I don't understand." His mom leaned forward.

"Well I guess I'm bisexual?" He gave me a questioning look.

I choked trying to suppress my laughter, gaining everyone's attention. Torin patted my back, but didn't even try to explain how he was only attracted to me in that way. It was way too complicated to discuss with them right then.

I was his and he was mine. That's all that mattered.

His parents seemed content with the answer because they were both nodding with thoughtful expressions.

His mom turned to me. "You won't hurt him."

It was a statement and I knew better than to grin or laugh.

"Mom," Torin began with exasperation but I cut him off.

"Never."

She nodded. "Well, okay then. I'll hold you to your word and, Torin, I expect the same from you."

"Never," he agreed.

"Good. Now, Torin, get back to helping me."

"Yes, ma'am." He saluted her when she stood and she swatted him with the towel in return.

"I guess it's time for me to head home and face my parents." I didn't want to leave, but I didn't want my parents left hanging with my confession, any longer than I had already when I'd taken off to come see Torin.

He walked me to the door.

"Want me to come?" he offered.

"No, it's fine. It might take my dad a minute to come around and it's probably better this way." He hadn't understood when I'd come out, but accepted it. However, he'd never contended with me having a boyfriend, so I didn't want Torin to feel uncomfortable if the conversation did go the way I feared.

"If you're sure."

I leaned in and kissed him again. "I'll see you tomorrow, and your mom said you better get to work making my cobbler."

He swatted my ass as I stepped onto the porch. "You'll be lucky to get any."

Blowing him a kiss, I left and drove back to my house, feeling calmer and breathing easier.

My parents sat at the round kitchen table, my mom rubbing my dad's shoulder and whispering to him. He leaned forward with his elbows on the table. I'd noticed my uncle's truck was gone when I pulled up and was glad I didn't have to involve him.

When I entered the room, my mom looked up, her long hair was in a messy ponytail and her hazel eyes I'd inherited focused on me.

"How serious are you and Torin?" she asked getting right to the point.

"Very serious." I settled in a chair next to Dad.

"And if you get drafted?" my dad asked, straightening and patting my mom's hand on his shoulder.

"He'll come with me." The thought of being separated by work didn't set well with me. Of course being separated by anything didn't either.

"He's okay with that?" He tilted his head and pursed his lips.

I nodded. "He plans to open an online shop and can do that from anywhere. That's what he wants. It was his idea."

"Okay then." He gave a curt nod and tapped the table with two firm thumps.

"Okay, as in, when he shows up tomorrow, you won't treat him any differently?"

My mom stood and rolled her eyes. "Of course we will. If you think we won't rib him a little, you'd be wrong."

I grinned. "Dad?"

He rubbed his jaw and cleared his throat. "I just want you to know I love you. I may not understand all of it, but I understand love." The truth about John, his brother, and the way my dad had stepped up for me and my mom... I knew he did understand it. He'd always treated me as if I was his real son. "If you say you love him, I'll believe you and support you both."

"More than anything." It was my one truth above all else.

He nodded and sighed. "I suspected as much."

"So you're good?"

He gave me a wry smile. "My son is happy. *Really* happy. I can see it on your face. So yes, I'm good. I'm proud of you for following your heart, no matter where it takes you." He glanced toward the kitchen where my mom had wandered, then back to me and I knew he was thinking of their situation.

As I watched my parents, I felt really lucky that circumstances had brought them together to be mine.

EPILOGUE

RUSH

THE STADIUM WAS massive compared to the ones we'd been playing in and packed to the brim. A large stage was the focal point and tables and chairs shoved together filled the bright green field. Jerseys from every major NFL team were hung side-by-side like a giant curtain. A mixture of smells from the various vendors competed with the deafening noise of excited spectators as they waited for the draft to begin.

I looked out over the crowd and my stomach turned with nerves. In my suit and tie, I sat at a table draped in a white tablecloth and surrounded by the people I loved. We all knew centers were lucky to get drafted, and a first-round pick had only happened ten times. Ten. The number was daunting. Not that I needed to go in the first round. Hell, I'd take any.

Though I weighed in at three hundred damn pounds of muscle, I didn't look like a typical center. I worried that would factor into their decisions as they weighed the benefits of choosing each player.

A raw memory increased my anxiety. After we'd earned

our spot in the playoffs, we'd been outmatched and our season had ended. I'd sucked up my disappointment and declared myself eligible for the draft. I'd gone to the combine and showcased my skills in front of coaches, general managers and scouts. I'd been pleased with my performance and hoped it had been enough to convince at least one representative that I was a worthy addition to their team.

Torin squeezed my hand under the table. "I know it's hard, but breathe. I've got your back." And he had. The whole process of entering the draft had been nerve wrack-ing, but exhilarating. So, as nervous as I was, I was also filled with anticipation. My future would be announced for everyone to hear. Though it was unsettling that I had no idea where this new adventure would take us, Torin and I had long conversations about making the best of wherever we ended up. His love and devotion eased my mind. I couldn't have done it without him.

I knew our friends were at home watching the whole event live. Doubts swirled through my brain, and I'd clenched my teeth until my jaws ached. I needed to calm down. It would be okay if I wasn't chosen. There was life outside of football, right? Or I could be a free agent. Above all, there was Torin, my rock.

My mom was a nervous wreck too as she sat wringing her hands in the fancy napkin on the table. This would make for a long damn day. The entire first round went by without my name being called and we returned to the hotel. I jerked my tie from my neck and Torin whispered behind me, "Come here."

Without complaint I turned to him, but instead of accepting his arms, I picked him up and tossed him on the bed before crawling my way up his body. I kissed him. With every touch I told him how much I appreciated him, but in case he wasn't getting the message. "Thank you."

"For what?"

I lifted my brow. Wasn't it obvious? "For being here and supporting me. I know I've been all over the place lately."

"It's a big deal. For both of us. You've worked hard for this day your whole life. Whatever happens affects us both, and I wouldn't be anywhere else. I feel you're counting yourself out, but you know some teams showed interest, so try to be patient."

"They were interested in a lot of players."

"Well there's only one player I'm interested in." He gave me a sexy grin.

I hummed against his neck. "Who might that be?"

He moaned when my tongue snaked out to trace his lips. "He's tall, solid build, hazel eyes, my best friend."

"He's a lucky bastard." I demanded entrance to his mouth and deepened the kiss. Pulling back I nipped his lip. "Shower?"

His grin was slow. "When have I ever said no?"

"Wouldn't matter if you did. I'd toss your ass in there."

"Then what are you waiting for."

I took him against the wall, his ass bumping against my front as I thrust inside him hard and deep. I wanted him to feel me the next day as we sat and awaited my fate all over again. When I'd left my boyfriend sated and sleepy, we crawled into bed and promptly passed out.

MOM AND DAD met us outside their hotel room, both trying to hide their nerves and failing miserably. "Here we go again," Torin said as we were shown to our table.

The place buzzed with activity, but now that most of the sought after star players had been picked, the insane uproar from yesterday had dulled to a manageable rumble where I could hear the surrounding conversation.

We waited for the event to begin. Time flew by and crawled at a snail's pace at the same time. The first team to go lit the giant screen to let us know they'd made their choice. The rep for the Texas Warriors came onto the stage.

"The Warriors pick Rush Jaggers, center from the Sugar Land Saints."

My mom squealed and tears filled her eyes. My dad slapped the table and Torin pumped his fist high in the air, screaming, "Holy shit, Rush. Get your ass up and go get your jersey!"

Relief and pride swelled in my heart as I noticed some other players watching me.

My face appeared on the large screens as I made my way to the stage. Someone gave me a hat to wear and I walked on stage wearing it. The feeling was euphoric as I shook hands with the rep and took my jersey, hearing the loud cheers of the Warrior fans.

"Welcome to the team," said the rep. He nodded and with a smile we both held a side of the jersey as a camera snapped our photo.

"Thank you so much." The happiness that filled my chest was nearly unmatched. Only one other thing had ever felt better. I sought Torin in the crowd, finding him easily as he stood, clapping with a smile that lit the room.

The rest of the day flew by in a haze. I couldn't wipe the smile from my face.

"Oh, honey, you'll still be close to home." My mom clapped her hands together and beamed a smile at me. The Texas Warriors was a best-case choice for all of us.

Torin's phone buzzed on the table.

"Hello?" he answered. As he listened, a slow smile spread across his face. Torin turned toward me.

"What's up?"

"Nash wants to know why you aren't answering your phone, and if now that you are some hot-shot NFL player, you're too good to talk to him."

Laughter burst free from deep in my chest as Torin held the phone to me. I took it and pressed it to my ear. "Sorry, it was loud, but it's quieted down some. I must not have heard it."

"Holy shit, Rush, you did it! You're in the NFL, not that we doubted you."

"We?" I asked.

"Oh, yeah. We have quite the party going on as we watched the draft. Say hi." Nash turned the speakerphone on.

"Fuck yeah, man," came from Shaw, and Bishop stated flatly, "Good job."

"It sounds like more than Shaw and Bishop are there."

"Oh the house is packed..." He trailed off. "Damn, who's that?"

Shaw growled. "Don't even think about it, Nash."

"What?" he asked.

"Rendon is off-limits. Stay away from my little brother."

"Hey, I had no idea." I could hear the load of bullshit in his tone and apparently so could Shaw.

"Nash, where are you going? You better not be... We have to go. Congrats, Rush. We'll celebrate properly when you get home. I need to go kick Nash's ass real quick." He rushed off and then the line went dead.

I glanced over at Torin who had crowded closer to hear everything.

Torin chuckled. "All he did was fuel Nash's interest."

"Yup, kid won't ever see him coming."

I'd only met him once before, but I agreed. Nash would chew him up and spit him out. Shaw was right to try to keep Nash away from Rendon. Poor guy.

Torin chuckled and leaned over to kiss me as if no one was watching. I pulled him close, wrapping my arms around him.

In about a month, Torin, my best friend and boyfriend, would walk the stage to receive his diploma, and I'd be there supporting him and loving him. Then we had plans to move closer to the Texas Warrior's facility and buy a house together.

Torin buried his face in the crook of my neck as I pictured us in a nice new house.

"Maybe we'll buy one with a pool." I let my imagination wander and held him tighter. *"Definitely a big yard."*

"Do you think we should get a dog?" I mused aloud.

I felt his smile against my skin. "Can I pick him?"

Chuckling, I kissed the top of his head. "No."

He burst out laughing and straightened in his chair. "We'll see."

We both knew I'd let him do anything he wanted. "Fine, but I get to name him."

He tilted his head to the side pretending to consider it. "We'll see." When I snuck a small pinch to his ass, he held his hands up. "Okay, okay, I think we should decide together."

The End.

ABOUT BAYLIN

Bios are challenging. I don't have a clue how to write about myself. Fictional characters? Sure! Me? Not so much. It's the reason my author bio stayed practically blank until after I finished my second novel.

Who am I? Well, I guess I should start by telling you that I write MM romance and I love what I do.

I fell in love with writing during elementary school with my first "Bare Book" but honestly never thought I'd become an author. It always seemed to be something I dreamed of and not something I could make a reality. Now that I have, I can't picture myself doing anything else.

I live in Texas where the heat and I don't get along. One day I hope to call Northeast USA home. I'm a wife and mother of two ridiculously cute kids. I have two dogs and one cat, the latter of which is a spoiled brat, but she's my spoiled brat.

Spending the day under a fluffy blanket reading or writing away on my laptop with a mountain of coffee is my idea of time well spent. I get to live so many lives through books that I consider myself genuinely lucky to call myself an avid reader. Books, whether I'm reading or writing them, make up a huge part of my life and I wouldn't have it any other way.

ACKNOWLEDGMENTS

This book wouldn't have been published without my incredibly appreciated support team.

Kid one and two, you better never actually be reading this. You two rock for understanding and finding ways to keep busy while I was stationed in front of my laptop for hours on end.

To my loudest cheerleader, my mom, you are probably the biggest reason my books see the light of day. Thank you for all your pep talks and all-around support.

Kathy, you know I couldn't do this without you. Thank you for everything you do.

My Crow's Clubhouse reader group, you all are amazing. It's nice to know I've got my own corner of the online world filled with readers and authors who support my work and provide a positive and fun atmosphere.

Thank you to the many authors, groups and blogs that help spread the word of Quarterback Sneak.

To you, the reader, I couldn't do this whole author thing without you. Thank you for reading, reviewing, recommending and sharing the book. It means the absolute world to me.

XOXO -Baylin

Made in the USA
Columbia, SC
12 May 2022

60318811R00071